PRAISE FOR

Sunnyside Plaza

"*Sunnyside Plaza* is a light in the shadows
that **illuminates the humanity in us all.** It's a
book as special as its characters. **A treasure.**"
—Jerry Spinelli, Newbery Medal–winning author
of *Maniac Magee* and *The Warden's Daughter*

"A beautiful book that **focuses on empathy, not pity,**
to introduce readers to a new world. **I enjoyed
every minute I spent with the characters**
of *Sunnyside Plaza*."
—Stacy McAnulty, bestselling author of *The
Miscalculations of Lightning Girl*

"**Pitch-perfect.** . . . Simon has given young readers **a
rare chance to celebrate the extraordinary courage**
of someone like Sally, and a chance to
understand where it comes from."
—*The New York Times Book Review*

"**Mr. Simon's respect and affection appear on every
page** of this gentle mystery. . . . **Earnest** and
humane, Mr. Simon's story **brims with so
much intentional kindness.**"
—*The Wall Street Journal*

By Scott Simon

LITTLE, BROWN AND COMPANY
New York Boston

Copyright © 2020 by Scott Simon
Discussion Guide copyright © 2021 by Little, Brown and Company

Cover art copyright © 2020 by Studio Muti. Cover design by Marcie Lawrence. Cover copyright © 2020 by Hachette Book Group, Inc.

Little, Brown and Company
Hachette Book Group
1290 Avenue of the Americas, New York, NY 10104
Visit us at LBYR.com

Originally published in hardcover and ebook by Little, Brown and Company in January 2020
First Trade Paperback Edition: January 2021

Little, Brown and Company is a division of Hachette Book Group, Inc. The Little, Brown name and logo are trademarks of Hachette Book Group, Inc.

The publisher is not responsible for websites (or their content) that are not owned by the publisher.

The Library of Congress has cataloged the hardcover edition as follows:
Names: Simon, Scott, author.
Title: Sunnyside Plaza / by Scott Simon.
Description: First edition. | New York; Boston: Little, Brown and Company, 2020. | Summary: While helping police officers Esther and Lon investigate a suspicious death at her group home, nineteen-year-old Sal Miyake, who is mentally challenged, gains insights into herself and makes new friends.
Identifiers: LCCN 2018050914| ISBN 9780316531207 (hardcover) | ISBN 9780316531191 (ebook) | ISBN 9780316456708 (library edition ebook)
Subjects: | CYAC: Interpersonal relations—Fiction. | People with mental disabilities—Fiction. | Group homes—Fiction. | Death—Fiction. | Mystery and detective stories.
Classification: LCC PZ7.1.S562 Sun 2020 | DDC [Fic]—dc23
LC record available at https://lccn.loc.gov/2018050914

ISBNs: 978-0-316-53121-4 (pbk.), 978-0-316-53119-1 (ebook)

Printed in the United States of America

LSC-C

Printing 1, 2020

In memory of Cecil and David Rosenthal:

"Moses' arms soon became so tired he could no long hold them up. So Aaron and Hur found a stone for him to sit on. Then they stood on each side of Moses, holding up his hands. So his hands held steady until sunset." (Exodus 17:12)

CHAPTER ONE

I CAN'T READ, BUT I LEARN A LOT OF THINGS. BRICKS are made of clay. Vitamin D comes from the sun. The sun is millions of miles away. There are 8 times 4 squares of tile on the ceiling of my room. I see that 2 times 8 plus 4 are cracked, and 2 times 8 plus 1 have brown stains. Smooth, strong, and satisfying. There are 4 times 8 plus 4 stairs from the third floor to the first. Venice is in Italy, but also in Ohio and Florida. Fast, fast, fast relief! Florida has alligators and crocodiles. They're not the same, but both bite. Snap, crackle, pop! Or your money back. Gets those hard-to-reach areas. Shirts have 8 buttons, but I button

7 because I don't button the top. I notice things. Today is April two-four and at six-zero-four in the morning I came down the 4 times 8 plus 4 steps to work.

I work in the kitchen of Sunnyside Plaza and live upstairs, too, on floor 3. There are 4 other people in my room—Mary, Pilar, Trish, and Shaaran—and Ray, Julius, and Tony next door. There are 5 people in the room next to us and 4 people in the room next to them. There are 5 rooms, too, on floor 2.

When I get downstairs in the morning, I always take 8 paper bowls at a time from the kitchen to the dining room. I do this 8 times, so there is a bowl for everybody and a few left over.

Conrad, the cook, was already in the kitchen. He has a big soft red face and a singsong voice.

"G'morning, Sal," he called. "Check the spoons, too, please."

The white plastic spoons were in a small steel tub. I counted 8 spoons 7 times, and then 6 more spoons.

"There is 1 for everybody," I told Conrad, "and 1, 2, 3, 4 extra." He sipped coffee and looked over at stacks of sliced bread.

"Ham sandwich lunch today," he told me. "I'll see if we have enough slices of cheddar, too. You like mustard or mayonnaise on yours?"

I made a face.

"I remember." Conrad laughed. "Nothing on yours, Sal Gal. Have some breakfast, dear, before they all come down. It's the most peaceful time of the day. Not a problem in the world can't be brightened by sunrise."

I live here because my mother got sick when I was in her stomach and then she couldn't take care of me. She went somewhere and hasn't come back. I lived in a few different homes and finally got here, to Sunnyside Plaza.

I'm 8 times 2 plus 3. My mother will be back when she can take care of me.

Sometimes at night, I wake and think I hear my mother in the hallway. I hear her voice—or hear someone's voice, and I'm sure it's her. I hear someone take a step and think it's her. I think she's just about to throw open the door. I hear her say, "Hey, Sal, let's get out of here!"

It's hard to get back to sleep. So I sing to myself, a song she sang to me and I still hear: *Hush, little baby, don't say a word....* I hear that song in my mother's voice.

My name is Sally. Sometimes Sal Gal, Sal Pal, or Sallie Pallie. It helps me feel like different people when I want.

Someday, I want to go to the North Pole, too. I want to know how to swim. I want a dog.

"Hey, Sallie Pallie," said Darnell. He was usually first for breakfast. "Cheerios here?"

"Picture on the box," I told him.

"Love my Cheerios," he said. "Little bitty wheels roll down my throat. Roll around in my belly." Darnell had a big belly, and he patted it like a drum to a tune only he knew. "Dah-dah-dah-da-dee, Cheerios going into me!"

And then Mary, my best friend, and David came down soon and poured some cornflakes. Then Julius and Tony and Pilar. There were 2 cartons of milk and 3 cartons of orange juice, and Tony shook cornflakes into a bowl and poured orange juice over them.

"Eeeew!" said Pilar.

"You're crazy!" went David, but Tony just said, "I like them that way. Corn and orange. Corn is orange. Orange corn."

"You are crazy," Darnell agreed. "Can I try?"

A red light from outside flashed and blinked over our tables. Dorothy, a nurse who worked all night, stepped out quickly.

"Just eat your breakfast, folks. I have to let in some people. No problem. Just enjoy your cereal."

The front door buzzed. Dorothy opened it. There was 1 man and 1 woman in dark blue who pushed in a small bed on wheels. Dorothy said the elevator was in the back, and the woman said, "That's okay. We can carry this. Let's just get up there."

We heard their heavy boots on the stairs. They whispered, but we couldn't hear what they said.

"I'm drawing a cat today," Darnell told everyone. "Like the cat I have with my mom."

"Bunnies better," said Pilar.

"People eat bunnies," said Isaac. He had come down to breakfast but just stood to watch the blinking red light outside turn around and around.

"Nobody eat my bunnies!" said Pilar. "I'll bite people who bite my bunnies!"

"I'm gonna make bunny Cheerios!" said Darnell.

Jimmy, who always wore an old brown army coat, always said "birdie" even inside where we could see no birds. He heard "bunny" and said "birdie" for the first time I heard that day.

We heard the elevator in the back of the house wheeze and grumble. A little while later the red light stopped blinking over the room. We heard voices of men and women outside, and then a car—what sounded like a big car—drove away.

A while later Mrs. Byrne, the nurse who ran everything at the home, came into the room where we had breakfast. Dorothy, too. And Bob, a nurse with a beard and glasses.

Mrs. Byrne's dark face was shiny, and she thumped her hand just below her neck a few times, as if that would help her get words out of her mouth.

"Is everyone here?" she finally asked. We all looked around. We saw the cereal, the milk cartons, and the calendar on the wall with pictures of kittens. I wanted 1 page to stay up all the time. It was a little orange kitten with white paws and a pink nose, asleep in a heart-shaped candy box. But then they had to flip the page.

Sometimes, when no one else was nearby, I flipped to that page and looked at that kitten.

I looked for Matt, Keesha, and Vy, who don't talk or move much but eat with spoons and look out wherever they are at whatever is in front of them. They were there. I didn't see Stu, Dennis, Laurence, or Charlene. But they usually came a little late because they got to the bathroom later.

Mary said, "Talia is still upstairs. She said she doesn't like cereal. She said she wants toast. She says—"

"I'll have to talk to her after this," said Mrs. Byrne. "And I don't see Marcus."

"Still in the bathroom," said Isaac, and a few people began to giggle. "We could hear him. He was going, 'Oh, wow, yeow—'"

"Marcus, too," said Mrs. Byrne. "I'll talk to everyone when I can. But I have some sad news, I'm afraid. It's Laurence. Laurence won't be here anymore."

There was a silence.

"His mother brought him home?" I asked.

"No," said Mrs. Byrne. "Not quite, dear, but in a way. You see, God brought Laurence home."

"God brought him to his momma?" asked Darnell.

"That red light—I thought it was God," said Mary. But I could see Conrad take off the white cap he wore in the kitchen and come around the serving table to put a hand on Mary's shoulder.

"Maybe I better start again," said Mrs. Byrne. "Laurence—he's dead. He died last night. In his sleep. The paramedics were just here and say it looks like what they call a stroke in his head, but Laurence was asleep. It was very peaceful, I'm sure. That nice man and woman in blue took him away. But Laurence— I'm afraid Laurence is gone. He's dead."

"Will he be back for lunch?" asked Darnell. "Should we save his cookie?"

CHAPTER TWO

AFTER BREAKFAST, WE TALKED ABOUT LAURENCE being dead while Tony and Mary and Pilar and Darnell and I worked in the kitchen with Conrad. I'd put down 4 slices of bread and plop a plastic spoon of mayonnaise on each slice and slide it around until the bread was wet and white to the edges. Mary pulled off a slice of ham and put 1 down each on 2 slices of bread. Tony would pull off a slice of orange cheese and lay it down on the other 2 slices. Then I'd flip the slice with ham over the slice with cheese and slide them back and forth until the edges matched. After 4 sandwiches were done, Conrad would put a hand on the top of a sandwich and slice the bread with a long knife.

"Why do you cut it across instead of up and down?"

Conrad thought for a moment.

"Because I think it shows a little extra care, Sal Gal," he told me. "Don't do just the least you can do. Put some extra care in it. But you always do," he told me. "You spread that mayo right to the edge. People get a little in every bite. You even up the slices. That's why I like working with you, Sal. You do things right."

I liked working with Conrad, too. Sometimes he told us stories about when he was the cook on a submarine.

"They had to like my cooking down there," he said. "What they gonna do—swim out to a hot dog stand?"

"I know lots of dead people," said Tony. Tony always knew a lot about everything.

"No big thing," he told us. "Some people are alive, some people are dead."

"But you don't see dead people, right?" asked Mary.

"They see us," said Tony. "They look over us all the time."

"Ewww," I told him. "All the time? In the bathroom?"

"They don't care," said Tony. "They're dead."

Mary pulled a slice of ham away from the pile and asked, "But where do dead people go?"

"Heaven," said Tony. "Up there."

"Up where?" asked Mary.

"In the sky," I told her. "Above—way above—the sky."

"Like…outer space?"

"Above that, even," I told her.

"Heaven is a place all with clouds," said Tony. "People sit on clouds, sleep on clouds, eat clouds. They look down at us and laugh, because down here, we need food, clothes, shoes. Up there, only clouds."

"I don't think I'd like that," said Mary. "I'd get cold."

"I'd like it," said Darnell. "Swimming through clouds. Looking down. Just floating along."

"Mrs. Byrne says we won't see Laurence 'cause

he's dead," said Tony. "Someone else will take his bed and clothes."

"Doesn't Laurence need them?" asked Darnell. "He's gonna wear clouds?"

Conrad began to pick up sandwiches, 2 at a time, and put them on trays.

"Heaven is your reward," he told us. "A reward for a life well-lived. It's eternal life. Life forever."

"I told you, dead people come back," said Darnell.

"Not exactly, Darnell," Conrad told him. "Dead people have lives up there. With God."

"I don't know God," Darnell pointed out. "Why can't I just stay here, with my friends?"

Conrad smiled and told him, "Well, my friend, I guess we're not the ones who get to decide when we go to our reward."

"A reward," said Mary, as if she was hearing the word all over again. "I can't wait for a reward."

But Conrad turned around with his arms filled with sandwiches, blew some hairs from his forehead, and said, "No need to hurry, Mary Berry. Make the most of what we have right in front of us."

When we finished the sandwiches for Conrad and he put them on the big table in the back of the room, next to the paper plates and bags of potato chips, I told him I had to go upstairs and use the bathroom. Mrs. Byrne was at our table and waved her hand for me to come over.

"You'll pass Laurence's room. Next to yours," she reminded me. "We have to keep it closed until some people can look at it. Okay, Sal?"

So when I got upstairs, I walked down the hall 8 times 5 plus 3 steps until I was in front of the room next to ours. Laurence, Isaac, Pam, and Terri slept there. Marc and Vy were on the other side. It was strange to see the blue door closed—nobody ever really closed the door at Sunnyside Plaza—and for a moment I wondered if I turned the knob and looked in, I'd catch Laurence, hiding. Maybe he'd be in bed, under the covers, playing a joke. Maybe he'd pop out his head. "Surprise, Sal Gal! Surprise, everybody! Surprise! Look who's here!"

But I was scared to turn the knob. I just stood in front of the blue door.

When I came back downstairs, Mrs. Byrne sat at the table with a lady who smelled like flowers. I began to walk by, but Mrs. Byrne put out her hand.

"Sally, do you think you could get a couple of cups of coffee from Conrad for us? This is—officer?"

"Detective Rivas. Esther Rivas," said the lady.

"You smell like flowers," I told her, and the lady named Esther let laughs burst out of her mouth. She wore black pants and a bright blue jacket. She had beautiful shiny black hair, like a bird.

"Well, thank you," she said. "It says, 'notes of rose and jasmine' on the cologne bottle. I didn't get your name."

"This is Sally," Mrs. Byrne told her. "Sal Gal, Sal Pal. Sally Miyake. Just next door in the hall from Laurence."

The lady put out her hand to shake mine. She smiled.

"Nobody says I smell like roses," said a man with a deep voice and who had a head that gleamed like a glass. He walked to the table from the hallway. "I'm her partner, Detective Bridges. London Bridges."

"Really?" asked Mrs. Byrne.

"Really. But Lon, usually." He held out his hand. "Nice to meet you, Ms. Miyake."

"What happened to your hair?"

"Sal!" said Mrs. Byrne, but the detectives laughed.

"I wonder, too. It just left me, a little bit at a time. Now I shave it all off, so my hats fit better."

"So where is your hat?" I asked, and Lon slapped the top of his head and said, "Darn, how did I forget my top hat again?"

Conrad kept a pot of coffee hot in the kitchen. I went through the door behind the table and fumbled to get 2 paper cups from a stack and put them down as I poured and listened to the voices outside.

"We have to ask some questions when someone dies alone," I heard Esther say.

"Of course."

"How did Mr. Fuller wind up here?"

"A birth defect," said Mrs. Byrne, then her voice got a little quiet. "Like most everyone else here. Oxygen cut off to his brain during delivery. He was born with his disability."

15

"And he came here...?"

"About nine years ago. He lived at home, but as his parents got older and had to take care of themselves more and more..."

I stopped pouring coffee when I heard Mrs. Byrne hold up on whatever words she had thought she would say. She finally told them, "Well, it's hard to care for a grown-up child at home, too."

"The parents are...?" asked Esther Rivas.

"Gone now. Both."

"Anyone to contact?"

"An older brother. We left a message."

I finished pouring coffee into the first paper cup and began to pour more into the other one.

Detective Lon asked, "Did the brother ever visit?"

"Now and then, yes," said Mrs. Byrne. "A little more recently."

"A little more?" asked Esther.

"I've seen that before. A younger sibling with challenges can take up a family's time. The older brothers and sisters feel overlooked. They hold a grudge. They have no contact. Then one day, their parents are gone, and they want to make things better."

I turned the corner with the 2 cups of coffee just as Mrs. Byrne finished saying, "I didn't know the whole story. I was just happy for them both."

"Well, me too," said the lady named Esther Rivas. She had long light-pink fingernails, but I counted 1, 2, 3 that were chipped, and 1 that wasn't pink at all.

I put the 2 cups of coffee on the table. Mrs. Byrne already had hers, so I put them in front of the detectives.

I asked them, "Are you married?"

Esther and Lon looked at each other—and laughed.

"No!" said Esther. "Not to each other. I'm married. A great guy named Robert."

"Sal…," Mrs. Byrne began, but Esther told her, "It's fine."

"Is he a detective?" I wanted to know.

"A lawyer. I put people in jail, he gets them out."

"They got both ends covered," Lon Bridges said. "I'm not married. I mean, Ms. Miyake, who'd ever marry a bald, smelly guy like me?"

I liked to hear London Bridges call me Ms. Miyake, so I told him, "I would."

17

That sure made them laugh again. Mrs. Byrne said, "Sal Gal!" as if she was upset by what I'd said, but she laughed, too.

I wanted to sit down with them but knew I should get back to the kitchen. Conrad wanted me to take apples from the crate in the kitchen and rinse them under water before lunch. I put the first 8 in the sink and under the nozzle and sprayed them with water. Then I turned off the spray to let the water drip and heard Lon talking.

"There didn't seem to be a lot up there when I looked. In his closet or table."

"They don't have much here," Mrs. Byrne told him. "A couple shirts, sweaters, socks. If you don't go outside much, slippers are fine. All donations. People get rid of what they don't want. Then they think of us."

"No letters, books? Cell phones?"

"Picture books sometimes. But our folks are usually with us because reading can be a little out of their grasp," I heard Mrs. Byrne say softly. "Some might learn to recognize a few names, numbers, or signs. Sunnyside, 36 Broadway. Or Cheerios, Santa, M&M's. There are lots of people with disabilities who can read, hold jobs in the outside world, and live on their own. Our folks are with us because they need a different level of care."

There was a long pause and I waited until Esther began to speak to pick up the apples from the sink.

"And do you know what happens to Mr. Fuller now?"

"Our notes in the office are for Laurence to be cremated," said Mrs. Byrne. "The funeral homes on Clark usually help out when…this happens. They've told us that usually no one comes for the ashes. That's why I'm glad it might be different for Laurence. He's got a brother. Lots of our folks at Sunnyside Plaza have no family."

Mrs. Byrne spoke a little more softly again.

"At least not a family that's a part of their lives."

I took the rinsed apples from the sink in both my hands, then put them onto the counter. Conrad tells me I should dry my hands on a towel, but it's easier just to wipe them on the back of my pants. I went over to the crate for more apples and stopped a moment when I heard Lon's voice, speaking a little louder.

I can't read, but I see, I hear, and I notice things.

"The medical examiner should be able to review everything this afternoon," said London Bridges. "It

looks like Laurence took a standard pill for choles-
terol. And…"

He seemed to take a slight breath, like before you
jump, before trying to say the next word.

"Tri…flu…oper…"

"Trifluoperazine, yes." Mrs. Byrne said the word
without a pause or stumble, like she was saying "chair,"
"cereal," or "water." "Almost every resident takes
something. It's hard to be as rambunctious as a six-
year-old when you're in the body of a twenty-, forty-, or
sixty-year-old. It's for their own safety."

Lon's voice slowed again.

"And…this…sele…gi? Selegiline?"

"Same. It calms them."

The back door buzzed. Conrad opened it and let in
George, the man who delivered cans of food to us.
He had a box in his arms and the cans clinked in the
box.

"Hey, how we doing?" George asked, and Conrad held a finger to his lips.

"Sad morning, George. One of our folks left us."

George asked, "Just walked out the door?" and

Conrad shook his head and lifted his hands up toward the ceiling.

"Out of life," Conrad explained.

"Oh, wow, Connie," said George. "Tough break. I'm sorry."

I had begun to bend down to pick up another 8 apples when Conrad said to me, "The rest can wait awhile, Sallie Pallie. Why don't you take a few out to our guests and Mrs. Byrne?"

So I filled my hands with 3 apples and went around the corner to the table in time to hear Esther say, "Forty-six. So young."

"But it can be prime for a stroke," said Mrs. Byrne.

"Believe me, we know," said Lon Bridges. "We had a guy in the Nineteenth District, about the same age."

"Thanks so much, Sal," said Mrs. Byrne as she looked up from the table when I brought the apples.

"Thank you, Ms. Miyake," said London Bridges. "May we call you Sally? Or do you like Sal?"

I felt a little hotness on my face.

"I love that," I told them, and then turned around to smile.

"Being a police officer must be stressful," Mrs. Byrne told the detectives. "Emergencies, sirens. Seeing

21

things most people don't. But living here can be hard work, too."

I had turned the corner into the kitchen but held up a step so I could still hear them.

"It seems so nice," I heard from Esther. "Sunnyside Plaza—an oasis of peace in the heart of the big, loud city."

"Oh, it is," said Mrs. Byrne. "But there comes a time, when folks here turn thirty or forty and realize…"

I took a couple more steps when I heard Mrs. Byrne stop and lower her voice. But I still listened.

"…realize they've kind of been cut off from things. The rest of the world goes to jobs, gets married, has a dog, cat, kids. They see all that on screens. They talk about it with each other. Then they look around and see that they're…here. For good. We try to give them good lives," Mrs. Byrne said almost in a whisper. "They eat, draw, paint, and help out. Musicians come in once a month or so, and they get to bang on drums. We take them to picnics, church concerts, Purim parties, Eid al-Adha, Easter Monday at St. Andrew's. We treat them with love. They have fun. They help each other. I see amazing kindness in them every day. But one day, most folks here realize that a whole big world is out there. And they're... here."

I heard Mrs. Byrne, I think, push back in her chair, then 1 more, then another.

I heard Esther Rivas say, "I guess that would get me down, too."

"Must take a lot of grit for them just to get through the day and try to be happy," said Lon Bridges.

I heard the 3 of them get silent together and knew they shouldn't know that I could hear them.

Most of us wound up in front of the television screen that night. A dog got lost but found its way home. A man fired a gun and blew up a car and everyone walked away. Low tonight five-four, high tomorrow seven-one, chance of rain around lunch. It's a big world, somebody has to furnish it. The Bulls lost. San Antonio won. A mother and father argued about something silly and realized they really loved each other. Made with whole-grain goodness. Cooler near the lake. Frrrrom Holllywood... Gets rid of fine lines and wrinkles. These engines can't take much more! And look—it vacuums tacks!

Matt looked straight ahead. I saw him lick his lips. Vy snorted.

Mark, a nurse who worked at night, came in to tell us it was time to brush our teeth and get into bed, and we did.

Jimmy said "birdie" one more time.

After Pilar, Mary, and Shaaran had gone to sleep, or pretended to, and Pilar had climbed in with Tony, I got out of bed and went to the window to look out. I could see the blinking red letters of a place we didn't know, the white light of the laundry wash all over the sidewalk; the yellow lights of the deli with people laughing and drinking in the window; the silver light of the coffee shop with people dozing and sipping; the red, white, and blue bus stopping and starting and 2 little kids looking out the big back window as it rolled down the street toward the lake and the stars. I notice things.

CHAPTER THREE

"I DON'T LIKE PEOPLE BEING DEAD," DARNELL announced in the kitchen the next day. "You can't talk to them."

Conrad was working to open a can of peaches.

"You can talk to someone who's gone," he told Darnell in a soft voice. "Just talk to them in your heart. They'll hear you."

"You want to say something to Laurence?" asked Tony.

"I want to tell him, 'Stop taking my socks!'" said Darnell.

"He won't take your socks if he's dead," said Mary. Darnell looked to Conrad.

"Mary Berry has a point there, Darnell."

"But you said he's over everything. I bet he tells Tony to take my socks."

Tony put his hands up to his ears.

"I hear you, Laurence! I hear you!" he said.

"You ain't fooling me, Laurence," Darnell said, looking up into the sky.

A man in brown pants, a smudged white shirt, and a rumpled black jacket was in the hallway outside the kitchen and the room where we ate when I went out to go to the bathroom. He looked at me and opened his mouth to talk before I could say hello.

"Excuse me, ma'am," he said. "I'm the guy here to repair the printer in the office. I went out to the washroom and got lost."

"Washroom" sounded like "bathroom" to me, so I asked, "You were in the bathroom?"

He smiled.

"I didn't want to say it like that. But yes. Now I don't know how to get back. To the office."

"Oh," I told him, and held out a finger. "Walk right there," I said. "It's a brown door."

"Thanks so much," he said, then took a step closer and spoke a little softer.

"May I ask—what kind of place is this?"

"Sunnyside."

"Yes, Sunnyside Plaza. Is it a hotel?"

"We live here."

"All the time?"

"Sometimes people go out," I told him. "We went to a fair. Shaaran went to the dentist."

"You're pretty funny," he said. Then the man in brown pants and a smudged white shirt got a step closer. He asked, "So...are the people here...sick?"

"Well," I told him, "Tony sneezed at breakfast."

"That's a good one." He laughed. "I mean, are the people..."

The man held a finger up to his head and wiggled it in a circle 1, 2, then 3 times.

I laughed, too, then I held my finger up to my head and wiggled my finger, too.

"Oh, I figured that," he said. He laughed, loud by now, as he walked down the hall toward the office.

Mrs. Byrne had come out of a bathroom and saw

27

the man in brown pants and a rumpled black jacket walk away. She heard him laugh and saw him wiggle a finger next to his head.

Mrs. Byrne just stopped.

"He shouldn't do that," she said. "Don't pay attention to him, Sal Gal."

"It's okay," I told Mrs. Byrne. "He's lost."

"I'll say," said Mrs. Byrne.

The can of peaches was so big and heavy that Darnell had to hold it with his big hands while Tony held on to Darnell, and Conrad picked at the top with a can opener. Mary and I got out the spoons with holes and a stack of paper bowls. We waited for them to lift up the lid.

Mrs. Byrne came around the corner into the kitchen.

"Conrad, we have a visitor. Can I have a couple of cups of coffee?"

Conrad nodded at me.

"This may take a while. Sal Gal, you figure you and Mary Berry can help out Mrs. B?"

I held 2 cups while Mary poured, and then turned around to take them out to the dining room because

Mary is shy. The lady who smelled like roses sat at the table.

"Ms. Miyake, right?"

I felt my face get warm again.

"Lon will be sorry that he missed you. I just came by to fill in Mrs. Byrne on a few things. Nice to see you. I'm Esther."

"I know."

"Think you can find some milk for us back there, too, Sal?" asked Mrs. Byrne, and I listened to them as I turned around for the kitchen.

"The medical examiner found nothing surprising, really," I heard Esther say. "Laurence had a stroke, like it seemed. They did some blood work, of course. Was Laurence on a special diet?"

I turned the corner and held still in front of the refrigerator.

"Everyone here is," she said. "Because of their limited mobility. We try to keep things low calorie, low fat, low sugar. Without cutting out all the fun."

"Cookies, I saw," I heard Esther say.

"Yes, for fun. And ice cream sometimes. And cereal in the morning, or else they'd never eat breakfast. But we count calories and fats. The chicken is usually skinless. The hot dogs are usually chicken. One dessert a day, except birthdays. It would be a good diet for you and me," said Mrs. Byrne.

I heard Esther's light laugh.

"I could use it," she agreed.

"In the summer, we get some donations of fresh vegetables and fruits from farmers. But usually only what they haven't been able to sell, so it's not a lot. Most everything here has to be canned, frozen, or come out of a box," said Mrs. Byrne. "Taxpayers don't want to pay for first-class meals here."

I turned the corner with a carton of milk, half-full.

"Yes," said Esther Rivas. "They like to get their cops at low cost, too."

I put the milk between the 2 ladies and began to turn, but Mrs. Byrne asked a question.

"You like the food here, Sal?"

"Oh yes."

"Sally helps Conrad in the kitchen. He loves our folks and does a great job. They rinse and wash and bring things out. Sally here even gets to chop. You have a good time in there, don't you, Sally? You and Darnell. Mary and Tony?"

"We like to help. It's fun."

"Well, Sunnyside is a happy place, I can see that," said Detective Rivas. She reached up and brushed a lock of her hair back from her eyes.

"I wish I could do that," I told her.

"What?" she asked nicely.

"Pull hair from over my eyes." My hair is short.

"We try to keep hair pretty short here," said Mrs. Byrne. "Easiest for everyone."

"I like your hair, Sal," said Esther. "Short and chic. French."

"Like french fries?" I asked, and we all laughed.

"Much prettier," said Esther.

The top of the peaches can was open, and Mary and I began to fish in the orange syrup of the big can with our slotted spoons. We brought up peaches, 2 or 3 slices at a time, like Conrad wanted, let syrup drip back into the can, then plunked the peach slices into bowls. We liked to watch the syrup drip, fast like a river at first, then long, slow drips that held up in little balls before they went plunk.

31

I heard Mrs. Byrne tell Esther, "Dr. Maddux comes every Wednesday morning. He re-ups prescriptions before they run out."

"Does he ever not re-up a prescription?" Esther asked, and I heard a pause that went on long enough to stop my fishing in the peach syrup. I wanted to hear the answer.

"You have to understand something, Detective," said Mrs. Byrne. "The folks here—our folks—don't get *better*. They don't get *over* it. They don't *have* something. It's who they *are*. There's no cure and nothing to get over. It's their lives. They have a right to be happy, and we help them."

"Well, that's important work," I heard Esther Rivas say.

Mary and I fished for peaches and plopped them into bowls for lunch.

A lot of us drew and colored in the afternoon, around the large table with a brown top on the top floor of Sunnyside Plaza. Raymond drew more cats, with round brown faces and red triangle ears. "This one is named Peewee," he said. "He's small and cute. This one is named Biggy—he's big. And this one is named Brownie, because he looks like a brownie with red ears."

"Your cats always smile," Julius told him. "But cats don't smile."

"Mine do," said Ray. "They're happy. They're my cats at home, with my mother."

Pilar had drawn a park with slides and swings and a dog in a swing.

"His ears look like wings, don't they?" she asked us all. "He can fly away. But he comes back, my dog."

Jimmy sat at the table and didn't draw. Matt didn't draw but kept a blue crayon in his fingers. Keesha sat in the corner and slept.

I heard steps and turned my head.

"Ms. Miyake." It was London Bridges.

I moved back my chair to face him and said, "Hi," very softly.

Mrs. Byrne came in alongside.

"We call this the community room," she said. "Painting, drawing."

"I'm Julius," said Julius. He had on his gray sweater

and put the green crayon in his pocket. Detective Bridges lowered his hand to shake Julius's.

"I'm Lon. Lon Bridges. Just taking a look around."

"He's a detective," I told the table.

"Oh, Ms. Miyake, you gave away my secret!" he said, and my face felt warm again.

"Detective Bridges wanted to see again where Laurence was," said Mrs. Byrne.

"Nice, comfortable rooms you got here," he said.

"My picture!" said Pilar, and she held it up so Lon Bridges could give it a good look. He looked at it from side to side and smiled.

"That's sure enough beautiful," he said. "That a dog in that swing?"

"Yes! Yes! I call him Rusty—that's how it sounds when it swings!"

"Well, Rusty is a fine-looking pooch," said Lon. "Brown spots, it looks like. He's a cocker spaniel?"

"I guess. I suppose."

"Lookit my cats!" said Raymond. "The brown one with red ears!"

"Never, ever seen such a fine feline," said Lon Bridges.

I smelled roses, with notes of jasmine, and saw Esther Rivas. She turned the corner and came into the room where we drew and colored on the big brown table.

"I know her," I told everyone.

"Look at my dog. In the swing," said Pilar as she held up her sheet of paper. "It's what it looks like when I'm at home and we're all in the park."

Esther Rivas scrunched down and looked at Pilar's drawing as she shook it in her hands.

"Yes. Yes, I see that," said Esther. "His ears. There's something about his ears."

"Yes! Yes!" said Pilar. "Rusty, my dog—his ears are wings. He can fly away!"

"I knew I saw something. I'm a detective, after all. But why would he want to fly away if he's with you?"

"Yes! Yes!" Pilar said. "He wants to stay. Sometimes he just flaps his ears on a hot day. Someday, he's going to come here and take me for a ride."

"Look at my cat Brownie!" said Raymond, and then held up his drawing. Esther Rivas leaned over and ran a finger along the paper.

"A red-eared brown cat. He'd be easy to identify in a lineup," she said.

"Not that Brownie would ever do anything wrong," Lon Bridges added quickly, and Mrs. Byrne put her hand lightly on London Bridges's arm as she turned to me.

"I'm going to take our guests downstairs for a few minutes, Sal Gal. Conrad is on break. Do you think you can get them a couple of cups of coffee?"

I hadn't drawn much—just rubbed the black crayon lightly over the bottom of the paper to make a street, with a few streaks of yellow and red, like I saw outside. Lon held out his arm for me to go down the stairs first.

Jimmy saw us go by, or maybe he didn't, and said "birdie" again.

The coffee had been in the pot a long time and smelled strong and a little sour. But I got 2 paper cups and poured out just enough, and turned out of the kitchen to put them in front of Esther Rivas and London Bridges where they sat at the table.

"I don't know if there's much more," I told Mrs. Byrne, and she smiled.

"I'm fine, Sal," she told me. "Conrad should be back soon. Why don't you wait in the kitchen and see if you can help him out."

I sat on a high stool in front of a counter to wait for Conrad. And to listen.

"Well, I sure learned a lot from our time with the medical examiner," I heard Esther Rivas say. "When someone is on medications like"—and Esther slowed down to say them—"Tri-flu-operazine and Sele-giline, certain things in the diet might help trigger what happened to Laurence."

"And as I told you," Mrs. Byrne said with sharp, hard words I knew meant that she was upset. "Every meal here is low calorie, low fat, low sugar. With treats to make life a little sweeter."

"Cheese, now and then," said Lon Bridges.

"A thin slice of cheddar, maybe once a day. We should all eat so healthy. In fact, I do—Conrad makes the same meals for me. Not even an extra bag of chips."

"Sourdough bread? Anything with a yeast that's aged?"

"Our food service delivers the cheapest white

or brown bread," said Mrs. Byrne. "Sometimes it's stale, and I tell George to take it back. He groans, but I won't stand for that. He acts like our folks can't tell the difference."

I could hear a smile in Lon Bridges's voice as he asked, "Red wine? Sauerkraut? Chicken or beef liver?"

"Not even in our dreams," Mrs. Byrne told him.

"Especially not in my dreams," Lon Bridges told her. "Liver and sauerkraut are nasty. We ask because some foods, if they're aged, can have something called tyramine."

"My partner knows this kind of stuff," Esther Rivas explained. "Tyra—the thing he said—can trigger headaches and even strokes."

"Dr. Maddux and I spoke as soon as we found Laurence," said Mrs. Byrne. "No headaches. His blood pressure was under control. Life—and death—happens," she said. "Even here."

"I've heard a few folks talk about going home," said Esther. "To dogs, cats, picnics, parks. What's that like for them?"

When Mrs. Byrne spoke after a long pause, she sounded tired.

"Detectives, most of our folks don't go home,"

she said. "It's a dream. To get them through. You saw Ray upstairs? He's in his fifties. His parents are long gone. Pilar? She came here as a teenager. She was in a dozen homes before that. Her parents were addicts. Do you think they're even still alive? That they have a big house and a nice pink bedroom waiting for Pilar? Even the few parents we know about don't come to see our folks here. They blame themselves. They don't know how to love them. They want to forget them. I'm not in their shoes. I don't judge. Julius? He's in his seventies and still draws pictures of cats like a five-year-old boy. Do you think he's going home to his parents?"

I heard the detectives say, "Ahhh" and "Ummm," but really make no answer.

"They talk about going home the way you or I talk about winning the lottery someday. And it's just about as likely."

There was a long silence—I stayed real still, so they wouldn't hear my stool creak or my shoes scrape the floor and know I'm listening—before I heard Lon Bridges say, "Well, they're blessed to be here, Mrs. Byrne. Anyone can see what a fine job you do here at Sunnyside Plaza."

Then I heard Esther Rivas say, "Shoot."

"Did something...?" asked Mrs. Byrne.

I heard chairs scratch along the floor and people start to stand.

"I'm sorry," said Esther. "I was supposed to go to a baseball game with my family—they should be right outside—but look at this, Lon."

"A ten-seventeen," I heard him say. "A little overtime today."

"My family—can they come inside for a moment?"

"Certainly," said Mrs. Byrne, and I heard her start toward the door herself. I came around the corner from the kitchen just as I heard the door buzz, the lock turn, and new voices rattle. There was a tall man with a kind smile and dark hair that had little sprinkles of white, a dark-haired girl who was not as tall and smelled like roses, and a little boy with shiny dark hair that curled over an eye.

Esther Rivas stepped forward and put her arms around the man, put a hand out to the girl, and kissed the little boy on the top of his head.

"My family," she said again. "My husband, Rob. Rob Bartlestein." The man smiled. "And our children,

Miriam and Javvy. Miriam Maria and Javier Bart-lestein."

Lon Bridges rubbed his hand on the little boy's head.

"Names like that, they're gonna be mayor and governor one day," he said, and the boy smiled.

"We're eight and twelve," said Javvy. "I'm the eight. My sister, Miriam, is so old!"

Mrs. Byrne said, "So pleased to meet you," and so I said, "Me too."

Esther dropped her voice to tell her husband about the ten-seventeen.

"I remember you telling me about that call," he said.

"Maybe it won't take long, but..."

"Yes, you guys have got to go. And now," said Rob Bartlestein. "Shame to have an empty seat for a game against the Cards."

"Mrs. Byrne?" Esther asked her. "Do you like baseball? You've been so helpful through this sad... situation...." But Mrs. Byrne had already begun to wave her hands like she was trying to shake water off of them.

"Oh, no, thank you. What are we—nine, ten blocks

away? And I haven't been to more than one or two. Thank you, but I'm here until six tonight."

So then I said, "I've never been to a baseball game."

Mrs. Byrne, Lon Bridges, and Esther Rivas turned around when they heard me. Rob, Miriam, and Javvy looked at me for the first time.

"Really?" asked Javvy. "Never never?"

"I see them on tee-vee all the time. They're on every day, and I like to cheer."

"Well then," said Esther Rivas. "Our boys need cheers. You've been so helpful, too, Ms. Miyake. Miriam, Javvy, this is Sal. Sally Miyake. She lives here at Sunnyside Plaza and works in the kitchen behind us."

"Pleased to meet you," I told them, and Rob Bartlestein stepped forward and held out his hand.

"I believe my wife mentioned you. You helped her a lot. I'm pleased to meet you, too."

I shook Rob Bartlestein's hand as he said, "So why don't you join us?"

We all turned to look at Mrs. Byrne.

"I...I don't see how it's possible. There are procedures. Forms to be signed, background checks..."

Esther Rivas lifted a side of her black jacket and

pointed a light pink fingernail at the gold badge she had on her belt.

"I'll vouch for him. And that's after fifteen years of marriage."

"You should have seen the background check her father ran on me," said Rob Bartlestein. "Sheesh. A prince of England couldn't pass his test."

Then Javvy and Miriam began to say, "Yes! Yes! Let her come!" and Mrs. Byrne smiled and shrugged.

"Okay then. A day pass. I'll go get the paperwork and you can be on your way."

"Yay!" said the kids, and Mrs. Byrne told me, "Sal Gal, why don't you go upstairs and get a sweater. You're going to have a great time with this family at the ballpark," and I ran up the stairs, into my room, to find my pink sweater under my other pair of shoes and yesterday's socks, and ran back down to join Esther's family.

CHAPTER FOUR

WE RODE THE BUS. IT WAS A BIG WHITE BUS WITH blue and red stripes and so many seats and so many people. It stopped and started, so more people got on and a few got off. I saw a man with a black wrap pulled over his head, a woman who wore dried flowers on a straw hat, a man who made sounds like a bird, and a little girl who hummed along with the whir of the bus. I saw red signs rush by, white words glow, windows gleam, and then I could see me: My face! My hair! My waving hands!

I could see me, reflected in the glass of the window, smile and wave back, like a moving picture, so when we rolled past a restaurant, I could almost see myself sitting there. What would I order? What would I eat? When we rolled by an office, I could almost see myself at a desk, or at an elevator. What did I do? What was my job?

When we rolled by an apartment building, I could see myself in the glass of the window, looking out the window at me, passing by on the bus and looking out from the bus. I could almost see myself sit on the rug in a living room, or the edge of a bed, and feel like someone who could look out at me on the bus, and wave back.

I told Esther's family, "I don't think I've ever been on a bus like this before."

"How do you go anywhere?" Javvy asked.

"I don't. Not really. I want to go home to see my mother."

"Why don't you take the bus there?" he asked.

"I don't know where to go."

"Oh."

"So you live back there?" asked Miriam.

"Yes."

"And work in the kitchen?"

"Yes."

"Wow," said Javvy. "Our parents don't work at home."

"They work at night sometimes, too," Miriam added.

"Things can happen at night," Rob Bartlestein told us all.

"I just work at day," I told the family.

"What do you do?" asked Miriam.

"Chop stuff. Pour stuff. Set out stuff. Fish for peaches and pears."

"Like fish? In the ocean?"

"In cans," I told them. "I fish for peaches, pears, and apples in the syrup."

"Can we do that sometime?" Javvy asked his father.

We got off with a lot of other people across the street from the ballpark. I saw the most people I have ever seen, 8 times many more 8s, times after times. I had to stop counting 8s. All different kinds of people, too: fathers and daughters, boyfriends and girlfriends, people in blue, people in red, people in T-shirts, grandfathers and grandsons, bunches of boys, people in pink, people in purple, people in jackets, grandmothers and granddaughters, people walking on heels, girlfriends with girlfriends, people in yellow, people in soft shoes. We walked through the gate and into a tunnel, which was very loud, with people laughing, and bright, buzzing lights, and strong, sizzling smells, and then through another tunnel, and out onto the other side to face a big beautiful green field.

It was as green as a park, and so bright I had to blink.

"This is beautiful," I told Esther's family, and Rob Bartlestein put a hand on my shoulder.

"It sure is. May I call you Sal?"

"Sal Gal, even."

"Is that a nickname, Sal Gal?" asked Miriam. "I've tried to do that with my name. But all my friends could come up with is"—and she paused—"bacterium," she said finally, and Javvy went, "Eeew!"

"I'm Javier, Lighter than Air," he said. "Javier I Swear."

"Javier, Who Cares?" said Miriam, but she laughed, then so did their father, and I laughed, too.

We sat down in a place that looked over all the green.

"So you've never been to a ball game?" Rob Bartlestein asked.

"Not like this," I told the family. "I've seen games on tee-vee. I've seen people play in the park. In front of Sunnyside Plaza, you see boys and girls walk along with balls and bats sometimes. Not like this."

"No, nothing is like this," he agreed. "Okay, gang, bring on those Cardinals," he said. "But first, are we a little thirsty? Lemonade, ice cream. And what about some hot dogs?"

"Hot dogs!" Javvy said all over again. "Hot dogs! Hot dogs!"

"I've had hot dogs," I told them.

"Not like here," said Javvy.

"I don't know what it is, but they're better here," said Miriam. "The bun is smooshy."

"Extra soft," said Javvy.

"I like the mustard. Tangy," said his father. "And the relish—green like a neon sign."

He waved at a man who had hot dogs in a big

silver tub and got 4. They were wrapped in crinkly paper and steam rose in my nose as I unwrapped it.

"This is sooo good," I told them as I chewed.

"We'll get something to drink, too," said Rob Bartlestein.

"And peanuts, too, right?" asked Miriam. "And ice cream."

"Not until the seventh inning," said their father. "I'm a strict disciplinarian."

I saw numbers on brick walls and on a big green board on the other side of the field and asked Rob Bartlestein about them.

"Oh. Well, straight ahead is the scoreboard," he explained. "The big dark-green board. Green, like an old blackboard. When a team scores a run, they put it up there. When a pitcher throws a ball or a strike, they put it up there. So even if you've been eating and talking and cracking open peanuts, you can look up at the scoreboard and know the story of the game at any second. Just by catching a glance at all the numbers."

"What's the 3 and 5 and 5 over there?" I asked and pointed.

"Oh, that's by the foul pole. Three hundred fifty-five feet to left field. Look out in the middle—four hundred feet to center. And over on the right, three hundred sixty-eight feet."

"Wow, all those feet?" I giggled.

"It's a way to measure space. I guess it probably comes from our flippers down here," said Rob Bartlestein.

Rob wiggled his feet, and then Javvy raised his to do the same, so I did, too.

"But your feet are bigger than mine," I told Rob Bartlestein.

"Well, yes. I've got real clodhoppers, as they say. Size twelves, like Frankenstein," he said. "Frankenstein Bartlestein." And then Rob Bartlestein opened his mouth wide to go "Ahhh. Ahhh." We laughed. Even a few people around us laughed. "But that doesn't mean left field is three hundred fifty-five of my feet away. Or your feet. Or Javvy's feet."

"My feet, then it would be, like, a zillion feet away," said the little boy.

"They settled on making twelve inches into a foot," said Rob.

"I'm four feet tall, right?" asked Javvy. "Four feet, ten inches."

"That was a couple of months ago, little squeak," Miriam announced. "I bet you're shorter now."

"Am not."

"Could be."

"Can't be."

They went back and forth before Rob Bartlestein announced, "Can't be. He's right. Your sister is kidding you. Are we here to watch the game? Sal Gal probably thinks we're crazy."

"Sal Gal likes you a lot," I told them.

I didn't know a lot about the game, but Esther's family helped me along.

"It's all in the numbers up on the board," Rob explained. "We're behind, three to two. It's the fifth inning. Can you see how many innings?" I followed his finger all the way to the left.

I told him, "8 plus 1."

"Yes. Well, yes," said Rob Bartlestein. "Unless we can get a run here, and maybe go extra innings."

I didn't quite know how to follow the game, but Javvy and Miriam and I made up one of our own.

"When the pitcher winds up, we can guess if the batter will swing."

I saw the man in the center of the brown mound in the field twist around, and as he threw the ball, I yelled, "Swing!" The man with the bat in his hand tried to swat the ball but missed.

"A point for Sal Gal," said Miriam. "He swung. Javvy?"

The man on the mound wound up again and threw. "No swing!" cried Javvy. The man with the bat did swing, but missed.

"Sal Gal one, Javier zero," said Miriam. "Dad?"

"I'll stay with balls and strikes," said Rob Bartlestein. "You go ahead."

Javvy had 4 times 8 plus 2 by the time we stopped, I had 3 times 8 plus 3, and Miriam had 3 times 8 plus 1.

"You win, little squeak," said Miriam. "But, Sal Gal, you were close."

"Pay attention now," said Javvy. "We've got a last chance here."

We had chocolate ice cream bars when they put two 0s under the 7 on the board and cracked peanuts through the whole game. I'm not sure who won, but I had a great time, even on the bus ride back, where we had to stand and people kept smiling at us and telling each other, "Hey, we'll get those guys tomorrow."

When our bus rolled by the street where we got off for Sunnyside Plaza, the whole Bartlestein family got off, too, and walked me inside. Dorothy buzzed the door. I showed them the kitchen.

"This is where I chop stuff," I said. "This is where I sprinkle cereal."

"Sprinkle," said Javvy, and laughed. "Sprinkle!"

"And this is where I fish."

"For pears and peaches," Miriam remembered.

Little Javvy shook my hand and Miriam kissed me and hugged me.

"What a great time, Sal Gal," she said.

"I'm sorry Esther couldn't join us. But I'm glad you could," said Rob Bartlestein. "She gets tickets to the games at the station house sometimes. I tell you what, Sal: Let's all go again soon. Would that be okay?"

"Yes. Yes!" I told him.

"Yes!" Miriam said. "We'll beat Javvy next time."

"Maybe you'd like to bring a friend along, too, Sal?" asked Rob, and I thought about Mary and Pilar.

"Yes. Yes!"

"Well then, we'll look forward to seeing you soon, Sal Gal," said Rob Bartlestein. Dorothy closed the door and I was happy to have such nice friends.

I saw Esther Rivas just a few days later. But it wasn't a happy time.

CHAPTER FIVE

ONE MORNING, I WAS ON MY WAY DOWNSTAIRS TO work when Tony saw me in the hallway. The door to his room was open, but the room still looked dark. Tony's face was red, and he looked scared.

"Julius" is what he said. "Julius, Sal Gal. Take a look."

I went into the room Tony shared with Julius, Darnell, and Ray. Darnell was awake and sat inside, but still in his pajamas. It looked like little ducks crawled over his arms. Tony was dressed in his blue sweater and tan pants, but no socks and shoes. He stood over Julius's bed. Tony's hands and shoulders trembled, as if he was cold.

"Look, Sal."

"Julius?" I called from across the room. "Julius?"

Julius didn't answer. He didn't move. Then I noticed I couldn't hear him breathing.

"Don't look at his face," said Tony. But I had to. I touched Julius's hand, just on top of his covers. It felt cold and hard. His fingers looked stuck together and didn't move.

"Julius," I said again softly, and then took a look at his face.

I had to turn away.

But before I did, I saw an eye, half-open and milky. His mouth was open just a little, and small white bubbles shined and popped in the corner of his lips.

"I think he's dead, like they call it," said Darnell.

"Did you...shake him? Try to wake him up?" I asked.

Darnell shouted from the edge of his bed: "Julius! Julius! Wake up now!"

I moved my hand to Julius's shoulder. It felt as hard and cold as the counter in the kitchen where I chopped.

"Maybe we should get Mrs. Byrne," I said.

"I'm still in my pajamas," said Darnell. "I can't go there in my pajamas."

"I don't think she'll mind," I said, and Tony and Darnell ran out the doorway, their bare feet slapping on the floor. A few seconds later, I heard them shout, "Mrs. Byrne! Mrs. Byrne! It's Julius! Julius!"

I didn't want Julius to be alone. So I stayed, and put my hand on top of his cold fingers, and looked into his cloudy eyes. I saw a crumpled towel on the end of his bed and put it over his eyes.

"Just sleep now, Julius. Have a good sleep."

Jimmy came out of his room, rubbing his eyes, his robe open, and the belt dragging over his toes. He cleared his throat to say "birdie."

I stood with Julius for a while and heard lots of voices and doors groaning open and snapping shut. Then I heard steps on our floor and a light knock and a deep voice.

"Ms. Miyake?"

It was Detective Bridges.

"I heard you were up here," he said softly. "You're

a good friend." He moved behind me and put a soft hand on my shoulder. "Why don't you say good-bye to your friend for now and join Detective Rivas downstairs? I've got a little work to do up here with Julius. And I think you can help Esther."

I walked downstairs slowly toward the voices I heard. I smelled coffee bubbling and rose cologne, and turned the corner around from the kitchen and saw Esther Rivas. She stood up from the chair where she sat at the table with Mrs. Byrne.

"Ms. Miyake. Sal Gal," she said. "Our children had a great time with you. My husband, too. I'm sorry this brings me back here so soon."

I began to cry. My shoulders began to shake. My nose began to run. I heard Mrs. Byrne's chair scratch the floor as she got up to put a hand on my arm and a napkin to my nose. Esther put an arm around my shoulder.

"I've never. Seen that. Before," I said between sobs. "Someone. Like. Julius. Is."

"It upsets me, too," Esther told me. "And I usually see strangers. Like that. You knew Julius. He was your friend."

"He lived a good life, Sal," Mrs. Byrne told me.

"A happy life, with friends like you. Remember his smile? Like an elf. Like an imp. He got to be seventy-three. Let's be happy today that he was around for so long and we knew him," she said. "I think the coffee might be ready now, dear. Do you think you could be kind enough to get a couple of cups for us? And maybe for Detective Bridges, too."

I wiped my nose, crumpled the napkin in my hand, and turned into the kitchen in time to hear Esther Rivas say to Mrs. Byrne, "Mr. Mills was seventy-three?"

"Yes."

"Well, God bless."

"Yes."

"No family you know about, I imagine?" Esther asked.

"Just those who knew him here," said Mrs. Byrne. "Julius was in one home or another since he was a teenager."

"Sixty years," said Esther.

"A ward of the state for all of that time, too," said Mrs. Byrne.

"Think of all the history he saw," said Esther.

"History doesn't really happen here," Mrs. Byrne told her. "News, weather, traffic. Who is president or mayor, what's the new music, basketball shoes, or hair-styles. Every now and then, somebody doesn't show up at breakfast. They notice. But our folks just keep going," she said. "Sadness doesn't weigh them down."

I came around the corner with 3 paper cups of cof-fee on a plate in time to see Detective Bridges walk through the door and stand near the table.

"Everything seems in order upstairs," he told them. "Looks like his time just came. Probably his heart. Nothing looks out of place. I closed his eyes and closed the door."

"The EMS team should be here soon," said Esther. "They'll take Julius. I'm sorry we had to come back so soon, Mrs. Byrne. On another sad call. How often does…well…*this* happen here?"

"'*This*'? You mean 'death'? You're being deli-cate, Detective. Not much. As our folks get sick, or begin to fail, they go to other places that take bet-ter care of them. We had a woman here for years, Juleanna. Bright, lively. Almost overnight, it seemed, she couldn't take care of herself. She was moved to a place that could. Then, I heard, she was gone. A few months ago, we had Miss Teller—Stevie, she was called, about sixty—who had sudden trouble walking. Took her to the hospital. Turned out she had a small stroke. Two, three days later…"

Mrs. Byrne didn't finish the words.

"We didn't tell folks here. They knew she was sick, saw she was gone, and just went on. It's the cycle of life, Detective," Mrs. Byrne told Esther. "Someday, you may come here for me."

"Well, not so soon, we hope," said Esther Rivas.

Tony, Darnell, Mary, and I counted out spoons and put out bowls just before people came down for breakfast. Detective London had brought down Tony's shoes. Darnell was still in his pajamas, but Mrs. Byrne had found a pair of white socks for him to wear so his feet wouldn't be cold on the kitchen floor.

"They're my socks," she told him. "From the gym."

"I can't wear girl socks!" said Darnell.

Mrs. Byrne laughed and asked with a smile, "There something wrong with being a girl, Darnell?

I'm a girl, you know. So are Mary and Sal. Sal *Gal*," she reminded him.

"You be girls, I'll be a guy," said Darnell as he held out the socks. "Nice and soft, though."

"For my dainty size tens," Mrs. Byrne told him. "Boys wear them, too. Socks are socks."

"Julius wears his socks to bed," said Darnell.

"Well, people get cold feet," said Mrs. Byrne.

"They're gonna take him away with his socks, aren't they?" asked Tony. "So his feet don't get cold."

"I'm sure," she told us.

After Mrs. Byrne had left to help Esther Rivas and London Bridges with the crew from the truck that had come for Julius, Conrad told us to take down the bread while he opened the refrigerator for the mayonnaise and the plastic packs of sliced turkey.

Tony asked him, "So, Laurence and Julius are up there together?"

"Oh, no doubt," Conrad told him. "Having their cornflakes together right now."

"Laurence liked the flakes with raisins," Tony reminded him.

"Well, maybe Laurence is branching out a little,"

said Conrad with a wink. "Up in Heaven, they're bound to have the best cornflakes. Best of everything."

He slapped down packs of the sliced turkey.

"Will they ever come by to say hello?" asked Mary.

"Well, maybe not in the way you're thinking, Mary Berry," he told her. "Not by walking in here and saying, 'Hey, how are you?' But in ways we'll feel, all the same. A memory. A laugh. Tell some old story, and they'll be right back with us in our thoughts."

Conrad held the huge jar of mayonnaise in his elbow and twisted the top.

"It's that easy?" she asked.

"That easy," said Conrad. "They're up there with my mom and my dad, and my old hound, Felix, and my old bird, Tweetie. And George Washington, Winston Churchill, Harriet Tubman, and Holy Mary, Mother of God."

"I was named after her," said Mary. "By my mother."

"She sure loves you, then, Mary Berry," said Conrad.

Tony began to shake slices of bread onto the counter and asked, "So Laurence and Julius are with their mothers?"

Conrad paused for a moment.

"Well, if not now, then soon. Blink of an eye. Really, it all flashes in front of us. A morning like this reminds you. Each minute goes by, can't be taken back. No time to waste."

"So stop talking and make sandwiches?" I asked Conrad, who told me, "Oh, Sal Gal, talking with your friends is never a waste of time."

"I can't wait to be dead," said Mary. "I can see my mother. I can have the best of everything."

"Oh, you don't want to say that, Mary Berry," said Conrad. "Being alive—it's a gift. We should hold on to it as long as we can, and pass it along to others. Heaven—that's a reward. We don't get to choose it. We have to earn our way there."

Conrad knew lots of things. He knew how to make hamburgers, fry potatoes, mix chocolate milk, scrape pans, and chop coleslaw. He could change the huge light bulbs in the kitchen, when they blinked out, and knew how to make all kinds of cookies, with raisins and nuts and chocolate and mint chips. So Mary asked him, "How?"

Conrad held up the plastic spatula he used to spread mayonnaise and told us, "Do good things. Make people happy. Take care of others."

Darnell had been scratching the bottoms of his feet, then stood up.

"What if I just want to stay here?" he asked. "I know I'm okay here. I get by here. I eat, I color, I help you, I play around. I get up there—who knows?"

Conrad sank the spatula into the mayonnaise and smiled.

"Well, as I say, Darney Chili con Carne, we don't get to choose. There's a power in life bigger than us."

"Bigger than Mrs. Byrne?" he asked.

"She's mighty big. But yes, bigger even than her."

"Wow" was all Darnell could say.

Esther Rivas spent some time with Mrs. Byrne in her office, and when she came out she found me in the kitchen.

"I wanted to ask you something before we left, Sal."

"Are you coming back?"

"Well, you never know," said Esther. "But what I wanted to ask was this. Have you ever been to a seder dinner?"

"No. I don't know. I guess not."

"For Passover. It's a holiday," she explained. "Like

Christmas is a holiday. Well, not quite like Christmas, I guess. It's when Moses led the Hebrews out of Egypt."

I didn't know any of that, really, but could tell Esther, "I've heard of Moses. And Egypt."

"Well, everything gets explained at dinner anyway," she said. "We have a family dinner. Family and friends. Special foods. We'd like you to come. Rob, Javvy, Miriam, me—all of us. Mrs. Byrne says it's fine. Would you like to bring a friend? Lon will be there, too. Detective Bridges. And his girlfriend."

I felt my face get a little red.

"Ferne is her name," said Esther. "She's very nice. You can tell her that they should get married."

My face felt more red and I smiled.

"Maybe Mary can come."

"The nice young woman with wavy brown hair? Of course," said Esther. "It's this Saturday. Mrs. Byrne says she'll make sure you're ready, and Rob will pick you up in a cab."

"Rob Bartlestein?"

Esther Rivas laughed.

"The same. The Rivas-Bartlestein household will see you in a couple of days, Sal Gal."

I got so excited thinking about dinner that I didn't think again about Julius for a while. It wasn't until Bob had made sure we'd brushed our teeth and splashed water on our faces, and Mary, Pilar, Trish, Shaaran, and I were on top of our beds and Bob had snapped off the lights and called out, "Good night, ladies! Sweet dreams!"

"I don't want to dream," said Trish. Our room was dark, but we saw lights from the streets and buses and stores outside, zipping and slipping across the window and our wall.

"Julius might be in my dream," Trish went on. "Trying to get out of being dead."

"You can't get out of being dead," said Shaaran. "You don't go back and forth."

"Julius's green sweater smells like barf," Pilar remembered. "Do they have to give it to someone?"

"It died before Julius," said Shaaran.

We laughed.

"Julius had that funny walk, didn't he?" said Pilar. "Picked up his foot."

"Like he was going to step on a bug," said Trish. "Cute little guy."

"I don't like all these people around here dying," I told everyone. "You get to know somebody, and they just die."

"I don't want anyone else to die," Mary told all of us. "Make it stop right now."

I watched a red bus light slide down the wall, like a glowing worm, and before it reached the end of my bed with my feet, I fell asleep.

CHAPTER SIX

W<small>E ALWAYS GET PILLS IN THE MORNING</small>. D<small>OROTHY</small> wheeled a cart to the small hall outside the room where we ate breakfast and people came out and knew to stand in line. Most of us have 1, 2 pills, but a few people have 1, 2, 3, maybe sometimes even 4 pills to swallow.

Dorothy looked at the paper on the tray that had our names and what we took, and began to say our names out loud. After she said our names, she gave us small paper cups with our pills and then poured a little water into a plastic cup. Then she watched us swallow.

"Sally Miyake," she said to me, and said to everybody, and then said a little louder, "Sal *Gal*."

My small cup had a white pill and a blue-and-white pill. I saw them every morning. White, like a cloud, and the other one, half-white, like a cloud, and half-blue, like the sky. I put the pills into my mouth and let them roll around and poured the water over them and swallowed.

"I just get a blue pill and a white pill," Darnell said. "Sal gets a pretty blue-and-white pill."

"Do you even stop to look at what you swallow, Darnell?" Dorothy asked him. Darnell gave a big, loud slap to the top of his tummy, like he was hitting a drum or trying to swat a bug. He turned the cup over in his mouth and laughed, then took a swallow of water to swallow his blue pill and his white pill.

Then Tony asked, "How do you know I don't get Darnell's pills? Or Pilar's?"

"As a matter of fact," Dorothy told him, "you and Pilar take the same kind of pills. But different doses. Dr. Maddux writes it all down. We're careful that you only get your pills. C'mon now, swallow them," she said, and Tony put the cup up to his mouth, let his pills roll in, and swallowed them with a gulp of water so big it looked like he had a baseball in his mouth, but he didn't.

"What happens if I don't take my pills?" Tony asked. "Someday."

"That won't happen," Dorothy told him. "I won't let that happen."

"Will I get sick?"

"Not as sick as you'll get if I see you not taking them," said Dorothy. "I'll get so mad you'll wish you were sick. And you'll have to take more pills to get over me getting mad."

"What if I just popped them in my mouth," asked Darnell, "but then I don't swallow them?"

"They'll melt," said Dorothy. "They'll get gunky all over your mouth, and then you'd have to swallow them."

"You win," Darnell told Dorothy. "You always win."

Dorothy turned back to the paper on the cart, but I could see her try to stop herself from smiling, or letting us see her smile, by holding a hand up to her mouth.

"Okay, Pilar," said Dorothy, and reached for the small cup with a pink pill and a blue-and-white pill.

Rob Bartlestein and Javvy came to Sunnyside Plaza in a taxicab, not a bus. The driver waited outside for Rob and Javvy to come inside and talk to Mrs. Byrne, while Mary and I waited in the hallway.

Mary wore a yellow dress that Mrs. Byrne had found for her in a closet. Mary looked into the long mirror in the hallway and twirled.

"Oh, it's so pretty," I told her. "You're pretty." I could see Mary's face begin to turn red. "Yellow like the sun. Or a flower."

"Or a bird," said Mary.

Then I stepped in front of the mirror. Mrs. Byrne had found a blue dress with big red buttons.

"It's from the church down the street," I told Mary. "They have clothes in the basement."

"Red buttons," she noticed. "Big red buttons, like big red roses."

"See the shoes?" I asked. They were white.

"You are so red, white, and blue," Mary told me. "I like to look this way. Don't you?"

I don't think I was ever in a cab before. It didn't stop for people to get off and on. It just kept going, past big windows in front of bright stores, and people looking out at the street over steam from cups of coffee while they chewed on donuts and their fingernails. The cab stopped in front of a brown building, and Javvy and Rob Bartlestein opened both doors for us. The brown building had a red carpet, and we heard a door buzz and followed Javvy up the stairs for 2 floors. Esther Rivas stood and smiled in a doorway, and the hall smelled of roses and jasmine and cake in the oven.

"Sal Gal. And Mary Gerrity," she said. "We're so glad you could make it."

"I can always make it," said Mary.

Javvy was wearing a white shirt and blue tie, like Rob Bartlestein, and then Miriam showed up in the hallway and took my hands. She was wearing a blue dress with a white collar that looked like clouds.

"This is my friend Mary," I told her, and Miriam held my hand and took me into a large room that was bright with light and candles and people smiling.

"Ms. Miyake!" I heard a deep voice, almost like the wheels of the trains that rolled by at night.

"Detective Bridges!"

"Oh, it's Lon by now, don't you think?" he asked.

"We've seen a lot together. And we're breaking bread tonight."

"Actually, everything but bread," said Esther. "We'll explain."

I felt my face get warm, and Lon put a hand on the hand of a pretty woman with dark skin and bright blazing eyes.

"This is Ferne. Ferne Green," he said.

"You should marry him!" I told Ferne Green, and as she laughed she patted her chest with her hand to catch her breath a little and said, "Well, London Bridges, Ferne Green. With names like that, don't you think we kind of have to be together?"

"You're both beautiful," Mary told them.

We met 2 people named Ken and Lucy, and 2 people who were Marc and Maureen, too. Javvy wanted us to see his room. It was packed with toys and bears and pictures on his wall. He took us to his window to look out.

"And we see the ballpark up here. So many people when they play."

"That was so much fun. It must be fun to see it up here."

"Sometimes, Miriam and I sell lemonade and cookies for people who walk by. A dollar a cup, a dollar a cookie."

Miriam was behind us.

"And everybody tells us, 'This is the best deal in the neighborhood.' "

Esther Rivas came in to show us to the table. It was a long, dark table, with white cloth mats and red cloth napkins, and white candles that were already burning and twinkling. You could see them shining on the bright white plates, and the glittery forks and spoons and knives. There were 2 big bowls with brown, crisp potatoes, and a big bowl with lettuce and tomatoes, and dark green bottles with something purple inside.

Rob Bartlestein sat at one end of the table, and Esther Rivas on the other. Mary and I were on both sides of Esther, and Javvy was next to me. Rob looked at us from his end of the table and began.

"I'm glad everyone could join us," he said, then bowed his head to us slightly. "Sally, Mary—you especially. Some of you might not know all the rituals here, so I'll try to explain. But remember: Us lawyers get paid by the hour, so it could be a long night."

Everybody laughed.

"One of the rules of Seder is that we all have to drink four cups of wine tonight."

People applauded, and Esther laughed.

"Sal, Mary," said Rob Bartlestein, "I know you're all grown up. But why don't you stick with the sparkling grape juice. Like Javier."

"Like me, too," Lon Bridges said. "I'm a sparkling grape guy."

"Great juice," said Javvy. "Hold the glass to your nose, and you feel the bubbles pop."

Rob Bartlestein had some papers on his plate and looked down as he talked to us.

"The Seder celebrates Passover, the story of hope over suffering. It reminds us of when the Jews rose up out of slavery and left Egypt thousands of years ago. It reminds us to struggle against slavery, tyranny, and cruelty. Tonight, we say to all who are hungry, lonely, or scared, 'Come join us. Come eat.'"

"And you'll bust a gut for sure," said Marc, and Maureen stuck her elbow into Marc's stomach.

"Sorry." He laughed.

Rob Bartlestein held up a glass of the purple wine.

"And we have this waiting for Elijah, the prophet, even though he may not make himself visible tonight."

"Elijah called me," said Ken. "He's not coming. He said to give me his glass."

Everyone laughed and Lucy turned to us to say, "My husband is kidding, ladies."

"We could tell," I told her. "He jokes a lot."

"I like that," said Mary. "We do that with our friends, too."

"Elijah is with us in spirit," Esther told the table. "Like everyone—grandparents, parents, friends—that we've loved and who have left us."

Esther then lowered her voice to tell me and Mary, "Like Julius. And Laurence."

"Yes, Julius and Laurence," I said.

"Diego, too, right?" asked Javvy.

"Our dear little mutt," Esther told us. "Little gray fluffball. We lost him last year. Yes, Diego, too."

"Maybe we should pour some wine into his old bowl," said Marc, and Maureen dug her elbow into his stomach again.

"Blessed are you, our Lord," Rob Bartlestein said a little louder now, "creator of the universe, who has given us the gift of the fruit of the vine."

I held the glass of grape juice to my nose, until I felt a couple of bubbles pop and tickle. Then I took a sip. It was sweet and made a tingle in my mouth.

"This is good," said Mary.

"*L'chaim!*" said Rob and Javvy, and Miriam and Esther.

"It means, 'To Life,'" Esther told us. "The most precious gift."

"Sal and Mary, have you ever had matzo?" Rob Bartlestein asked. He held up a huge cracker.

"That's a big cracker," I told him.

"It sure is," said Rob. "That's because the Jews were in a big hurry to leave Egypt. They'd called down all kinds of plagues on Pharaoh—the king—and he was mad."

"Pissed. Royally," said Ken.

"So their bread didn't have time to rise. They took it out, flat. We call it the bread of affliction."

"Because it afflicts your mouth," said Ken.

"Matzo is good for you," said Lucy. "Or at least, not bad for you, like almost everything else. And now they make onion, whole wheat, gluten free...."

"Free the glutens!" cried Maureen.

"And if matzo isn't quite to your taste...," Esther Rivas told everyone, and lifted a red napkin from a bright yellow straw bowl. I smelled something I recognized.

"Tortillas!" said Javvy.

"Well, they're flat, too, aren't they?" said Esther.

"We praise you, God, for tortillas!" said Miriam, and everyone at the table, including Mary and me, went, "Amen—tortillas!"

Miriam held up a square box and shook it.

"Look," she said. "I can't believe it. These matzos were baked in...*New Jersey*!"

"Eeew!" said everyone, as if someone had taken off their shoes and put their feet on the table. "Eeew!"

"We can't make good matzo, right here?" asked Ken.

"Better matzo than New Jersey, anyway," said Lon Bridges.

"It's right here on the label," said Miriam, reading

from word to word. "One hundred calories...lactose free and vegetarian...wheat flour, water, apple cider, whole eggs, and..." She slowed down to drop her voice, so it was low and slow. "Newark, New Jersey. The label tells the story."

"Like a scoreboard," I said, and Javvy and Rob Bartlestein got excited.

"Yes! Hey! Like runs and hits!" said Javvy.

"Well, that brings us to the story of tonight," Rob Bartlestein went on. "A long time ago, the Jewish people were slaves in Egypt. The Pharaoh worked them to the bone to build his cities. And Pharaoh and his thugs—"

"Bad guys," Miriam whispered to me and Mary.

"—began to drown Jewish babies."

"That's terrible," I said. "That's so terrible."

"So one day," Rob went on, "a baby was born to a Hebrew lady. She already had a daughter named Miriam"—and then Rob Bartlestein paused to smile at Miriam—"for whom our own wonderful Miriam Maria Bartlestein is named. She didn't want her baby brother drowned. So she watched as her mother placed the little boy in a basket..."

"Like this one, I suppose," Esther Rivas said as she lifted the yellow tortilla basket.

"...and put it in the stream. Miriam knew the baby in the basket—her brother—would float down to where Pharaoh's daughter and her attendants splashed and frolicked."

People at the table laughed at that word.

"Teenagers frolic," said Rob. "Laugh, gossip, sing. Pharaoh's daughter saw the cute little baby. She fell in love and decided to adopt him. She named the baby Moses."

"So why am I not named Moses?" Javvy asked.

"It came up," said Esther. "*Moises*, it would have been," and little Javvy made a face like he'd just bitten into a bad pickle.

"Should we change it?" she asked.

"Nooo thanks!" Javvy told her.

"*Moses*," Rob Bartlestein repeated, "grew up as a prince of Egypt. But one day, God appeared to Moses in a burning bush."

"I know this story!" said Mary. "I've seen it, I think."

"And God gave Moses the Ten Commandments."

"I think you're mushing a couple of parts to-gether, darling," Esther Rivas told Rob Bartlestein. "But go on."

"The great part is coming up," said Miriam.

"It's all great," I told them.

"Moses told Pharaoh, 'Hey, bro. Let my people go.' But Pharaoh wouldn't hear of it. So God sent down plagues on them—"

"Plagues," said Ken. "Real horsesh—"

"Ken!" Lucy sort of shrieked. "Children!"

"Doo-doo, then," he said. "Bad stuff."

"I know the word 'crapola,'" Javvy announced.

"No need to show off here, darling," Esther told him, but she smiled.

"Locusts, hail, lice," said Rob Bartlestein, in a low, steady voice. "Frogs falling from the sky—imagine. Finally, Pharaoh said, 'Get out of here, Hebrews, you're killing me!' That's when they baked their matzo and tortillas and took off. But Pharaoh had second thoughts. He sent his soldiers. The Hebrews got to the Red Sea. The Egyptian legions were just about to drown them, when Moses raised his staff—"

"He called upon the Lord," said Esther.

"And God made the waters of the Red Sea part."

"Isn't that cool?" asked Miriam.

"The Hebrews escaped, with all their families and flocks," said Rob Bartlestein. "But then the Red Sea closed. The Egyptian soldiers drowned."

"Glub, glub, glub," said Marc.

We were all silent for a moment, and then London Bridges began to sing:

When Israel was in Egypt land, oppressed so hard they could not stand, God said, "Go down, Moses, way down in Egypt land. Tell ol' Pharaoh, to let My people go!"

"That's so beautiful!" I told Lon—really, I told everyone. "So beautiful!"

"We should have just asked Lon to sing the story," said Esther Rivas.

"Where did everyone go?" Mary asked.

"Here, for one place," said Rob Bartlestein. "And Milwaukee. Paris. New Jersey. All over the world."

"Because the world kept throwing us out," said Lucy. "Or worse."

"Like folks had to run away from Ireland," said Maureen.

"My folks got ripped out of Senegal," said Lon Bridges.

"Mine were captured in Gambia," said Ferne Green.

"Mine beat it out of Russia," said Lucy. "Just a step ahead of that Pharaoh's army."

"My folks had to hike out of Oaxaca," said Esther Rivas. "Hunger was their Pharaoh." And her face got soft and even more beautiful. "My grandfather got here in December and said he'd never seen anything as magical as snow."

"You get over that by January," said Marc.

Boy, there was a lot to eat. We ate so much. There were those big brown crunchy potatoes, and fluffy yellow rice, and chicken that was orange and sweet and fell off the bone in soft strings that we stuffed into tortillas with rice and raisins. There were some vegetables, too.

"Julius and Laurence would like this," Mary said. People smiled at us and stopped talking for a second, then began to talk and eat and laugh again. Mary and me, too.

We were eating and chewing and laughing when

we heard a "Whooo…Whooo…" from behind. Mary and I turned around. There was a bulge talking from under a white tablecloth. "Whooo…Whooo…," the bulge said again. It also wore white running shoes. "I'm…Elijah!" said the bulge. "Who drank my wine?"

Everyone at the table laughed, and the bulge shook off the white tablecloth.

"Javvy!"

"No—Elijah!" he said.

"Well, you sure look like my son, Javier," Esther Rivas told him.

"You are the mother of a prophet," said Lucy. "I'm not surprised."

"There's another little ritual we have," Rob Bartlestein said. "Just before dessert. Before you folks got here, Esther and I hid half a piece of matzo."

"You're going to be hungry after all this?" said Marc.

"It's a tradition," said Rob. "All the children at the table go through the apartment and try to find it. She—or he—who does gets extra whipped cream on her—or his—salted caramel cheesecake."

Esther held up one of the bright red napkins.

"When this flag hits the table," she announced, "the search begins!"

"Hint! Give us a hint!" said Javvy.

"It could be in the kitchen," said Esther. "Or, maybe the living room. Maybe right here in the dining room. But not in a bedroom or closet," she said, "so please don't look there."

"Bathroom?" asked Javvy.

"I wish I'd thought of that," said Esther. "Maybe next year. Three, two, one," she said, and dropped the napkin. "Find that matzo!"

Javvy ran from the table and turned down a hallway. Miriam got up slowly, with a slow smile, and walked into the living room.

Then Javvy ran back into the dining room.

"Not in the living room."

"Or the hallway," said Miriam, who had heard us, too. "You outdid yourself, Mamacita," she told Esther.

"Javvy. Darling," said Esther Rivas. "Since you're up, could you bring Sally and Mary the orange juice?"

"We're not giving up, are we?" he asked.

"No, dear. Just taking a break. A nice, refreshing orange juice break," she said.

Javvy walked into the kitchen. We heard the refrigerator door open. We heard things in the refrigerator being moved around. Then we heard Javvy.

"It's here! I found it! The refrigerator! I found it!"

Javvy ran into the dining room and everyone clapped.

"Way to go, Javier!" said Lon Bridges.

"You make the grade, Detective, first class," said Ferne Green.

"Beat me again, little bro," said Miriam.

But Javvy stopped.

"Orange juice," he said. "For Mary and Sal. I forgot it. Sor-r-ry!"

Javvy ran back into the kitchen. We heard the refrigerator open again.

Esther Rivas leaned over to say softly, almost like a whisper, to Mary and me, "He forgets about you, then remembers you," she said. "He treats you like sisters." And Mary and I grinned and grinned, but turned our heads to be sure Javvy didn't see us.

We were back at our place and in bed, with the plate of brownies and cookies Esther sent us back with on the small table between us, when Mary said, "I think that's the most fun I ever had. No one thing. Just being there."

"Me too," I told her, and soon fell asleep listening to the gassy buses starting and stopping in the dark night between the lights along the street outside Sunnyside Plaza.

CHAPTER SEVEN

THE BUZZER AT THE BACK DOOR BUZZED THE NEXT morning. Conrad said, "That's George." He opened the door and George was there, behind 1, 2, 3 boxes of peaches, apples, and pears in cans. I could see them on the labels. He had a little boy with him, with curly dark hair and big brown eyes.

"Morning, Connie," said George.

"Looks like a special visitor today," said Conrad. The little boy smiled.

"Chris, my boy," said George. "He's ten. No school today. Teacher's conference. Two months off during the summer isn't enough time for the teachers to have a conference? Anyway, I brought him along."

"He's a big help for sure," said Conrad. "I can see that. How goes it, Chris?"

Chris looked shy, but he smiled. George rolled in the boxes of cans. They clinked over each tile on the floor, apples clinking next to peaches, pears clinking on the edge of the brown cardboard box.

"Maybe Chris would like a little cereal?" asked Conrad. "We have cornflakes, Cheerios, Raisin Bran, and those wheat thingies," he said. "Or maybe a glass of milk? Come by for lunch, and we'll have cookies for you."

Conrad turned to me.

"Good cookies, too. Sal Gal—Sally here—helps make them. What's your favorite, Sal?"

I thought and thought, and then I said, "Chocolate chip. Chips stick on my teeth, but I lick them off."

I could see the little boy smile. It was almost a laugh. I like to make people laugh.

"I'm fine," he said.

George reached into the pocket of his blue jacket with his hand. There was a loud sound of paper crumpling and rumpling. George took out a clump of pink and blue papers and rubbed out wrinkles with his fingers.

"Some crazy problem," George said. "The wrong code or something on the billing for the cans. Mrs. B should take a look."

"I'll bring you back there," Conrad told him. "Sal, take care of things a minute, can you? Make our guest welcome."

Conrad and George turned the corner and I heard them begin to walk down the hall to see Mrs. Byrne. Chris looked at me and took a step back and turned down his mouth.

"I can get you some milk," I told him.

The little boy shook his head.

Then he asked, "You live here?"

"Yes," I told him. "I live here and work here and hang out here."

"Oh," said Chris. "And you're okay?"

"I'm okay," I told him. "I'm fine."

"My dad says there's something wrong with people here."

"I had a cold when it was cold out," I told Chris. "I'm fine now."

"My dad says the people here can't understand me, so I shouldn't talk to you."

"I understand you," I told the little boy. "Not every word, or everything all the time. But I understand people."

The little boy opened his eyes wide. We both heard George and Conrad as they came back in the hallway, walking and laughing. Chris shook a little. I told the little boy, "I won't say anything."

George and Conrad turned the corner, still laughing. I turned away from the little boy and began to wipe down the smooth steel counter behind me.

I know more than I can say. I know things I don't know how to say. Even if I have heard words and know them, I can't always say them. Sometimes it feels like I have a rock inside that sits on words. But I hear things and see things. I notice and figure out things. It's all here, inside.

We were making sandwiches in the kitchen a few days later when Conrad lifted up a ham and cheese sandwich with mustard and asked, "These things are pretty portable, aren't they?"

Mary, Darnell, Tony, Pilar, and I didn't know the word.

"Portable," Conrad repeated. "Small, light, easy to carry."

"I'm not portable," said Darnell, and Conrad laughed.

"Not hardly, Darney Barney. But you got two big ol' feet to get yourself around. You're what they call semiportable. I was just thinking," Conrad went on. "The weather looks good. You folks have been through a lot here, losing folks and friends. What say I talk to Mrs. Byrne and see if we can go to the park and have a picnic? Just eat lunch out there."

We cheered and clapped and rang the pans in the kitchen like bells.

Mark and Dorothy and Bob, the nurses, lined us up in pairs along the sidewalk.

"Hold hands, two by two!" Bob said. "Like Noah's Ark."

I held hands with Mary. Darnell was told to hold

hands with Tony, and he said, "I don't want to hold hands with Tony."

Dorothy let out a long breath.

"Okay. Then hold hands with..." Dorothy looked around. "Stephen," she said.

"I don't like Stephen," Darnell said. "He's on the first floor. I don't know him. Tony is my best friend."

"Then hold hands with him," said Dorothy.

"He's my friend, but he doesn't wash his hands," said Darnell.

Dorothy had one of those little envelopes with a wet tissue inside that smells like lemons. She opened it and handed the tissue to Tony, who liked how it smelled and wiped it under his nose with his hands.

"He'll have clean hands now, too," Dorothy told Darnell.

"But they'll smell like lemons. So will mine. I don't like lemons."

"Then don't eat your hands, Darnell," she said. "It will wear off before we have our sandwiches."

Bob counted us of by 2, 4, 6, 8, and a few more. "Sunnyside Plaza-ites, tallyho!" he shouted, and we began to walk toward the park. We walked by windows with red letters and pictures of fish and pictures of hot dogs and windows with people sipping out of cups and looking back at us.

Mary and I liked to look at people along the street. We'd smile and say hello, and some people would smile back. But a lot of people along the street would just stop and look at us, very hard. Like they didn't know what they were seeing, or thought something was wrong.

We got to the park. It was like stepping into a big green sea. The trees were like boats, and the leaves were like people on the deck of the boat who waved at us.

Bob and Mark put down the bags of sandwiches, and then Mary noticed and cried out, "Conrad!" He wore blue jeans, and a short red shirt, and a light blue cap with a red letter on it. We were amazed to see Conrad could wear blue jeans. We always saw Conrad in white pants, and a white kitchen shirt, and his white cap. But it was still Conrad. He carried a white cooler in his arms and jiggled it up and down. We could hear ice cubes slosh inside.

"You're gonna like this, folks" is all he said.

Dorothy had white laundry bags and began to pass them out.

"Pick a partner," she told us. "We're going to have races."

"I can't run with a bag over my head," said Darnell, and Dorothy laughed.

"No, sir," she said. "You put one leg in it, and your partner puts one of theirs in, too."

"Then how are we supposed to run?" Darnell asked. "With our legs in a bag."

"That's what makes it a good game," she said. Dorothy and Conrad each put a foot in a sack and began to run.

"You got to get coordinated," she said, and they took a few steps and fell down, rolling around and laughing.

I took a bag with Mary, Pilar took a sack with Tony, and Shaaran took a bag with Darnell. Dorothy and Conrad fell down again. Mark and Bob laughed so hard they couldn't run. Mary and I were ahead, but then we stumbled on our legs in the bag and fell over, too. Pilar and Tony were the first to get to the tree, and Bob jumped out of his bag with his arms up and cried, "The winner and world champions, Pilar and Antonio!" But we also ran a few more races, and Mary and I won one, too.

We stopped for lunch. Bob and Mark took the sandwiches out of paper bags and handed them out.

They were ham with orange cheese, and Bob lifted the edge of the slice on top to make sure mine had no mayonnaise, no mustard, no butter, or anything else.

Conrad jiggled the white cooler again.

"And here we have...," he said, then lifted the top, "lemonade!"

I had lemonade a few times before and usually don't like it much. But I liked these little cans of lemonade a lot. It was fun to sit in the sun on the grass and eat outdoors, and see people playing and running and riding bicycles, and dogs jumping and kids throwing and running after balls, and just not look at the same old walls.

Tony and Darnell went over to Conrad and said, "Thanks, Conrad."

"Thank Mrs. Byrne," he said. "She said, 'Yes, the folks could use a little pick-me-up, I'm sure.'"

"But you thought of it, Conrad," Darnell told him.

"Well, it's fun for me, too, Swell Darnell," he said. "I like to hear you laugh."

We were all putting our legs into our bags for another race when Mary looked up and saw 2 friends.

"Detective Rivas! Detective Bridges!"

They were walking down over a small hill beside

the street, and each of them carried small blue puffy bags.

"We heard there was a picnic," said Lon Bridges. "We didn't want to miss out."

"And we figured these might help," said Esther Rivas, and she unzipped the top of her puffy blue bag.

Shaaran recognized what was inside.

"Popsicles!" she said.

"Red and orange and green," Lon Bridges told us. "Who knows what flavors?"

We all sat on the grass, laughing and slurping.

"Javvy and Miriam say hello," Esther told us. "They want you to help search for Easter eggs."

"Ferne and I will be there, too," said Lon. "It takes two detectives to track down all the eggs."

"We'll go anywhere with you," Mary said immediately.

"I also thought," said Lon Bridges, "I'd ask Mrs. Byrne if Darnell and Tony could join me and Ferne at church on Easter, then help out in the egg hunt at Esther and Rob's."

"Darnell will be great to find the eggs," I told them. "If he can eat them."

We looked over to find Darnell and Tony and saw

that Darnell had walked a little bit away from our group to pick up a ball that a little girl in the park had kicked and run after. Darnell picked up the ball and tossed it up in the air toward the girl. A really excited adult—it must have been her mother—came running up within a few feet of Darnell.

"Okay, we've got it. Thank you. Just stay where you are."

Darnell looked puzzled. No, he looked hurt.

"I was just—"

"Yes, I know. We have the ball. Thank you."

She took her little girl by the arm. Esther and Lon had gotten up from the grass and were walking over to Darnell. The little girl stumbled on her legs to keep up with her mother pulling her. Her mother said, "Stay away from those people, Melissa. They're crazy."

Lon Bridges put a hand on Darnell's back and said, "Come back over with us, Darnell."

"Do you want Popsicles?" Darnell shouted toward the little girl and the lady. "They're good. We have red and green ones left. And lemonade."

"This is a fine man here," Lon told the lady in a loud voice. "These are great people here. You'd like them."

The lady began to run with her little girl. Esther came up behind Darnell and London Bridges.

"Don't worry, I'm not crazy!" Darnell shouted.

"She's crazy," Lon Bridges told Darnell. "Doesn't know nice people when she sees them."

"I'm not crazy, am I?" Darnell asked. And I could see his eyes get wet and red.

"You certainly are not," said Esther Rivas. "That lady is just worried about her daughter. She just doesn't know. And," she added, "she's a butthole."

London Bridges began to fall down laughing. Darnell laughed the tears right out of his eyes. Mary asked Lon and Esther, "What's a—what did you say? What's that word? Why is everybody laughing?"

Mary and I still laughed about all that—the races, the picnic, the Popsicles, the little girl, the crazy mother, and Esther's word—on our way down the stairs to begin work in the kitchen the next morning.

"That was funny," she said. "What hole? What's that word again?"

"I forgot," I told her.

"You remembered it last night," Mary remembered.

"But I told Esther I'd forget it as soon as we got back here."

Mary giggled.

"Darnell—he'll remember it."

"Did you hear him in his room last night?" I asked her. "He was singing it. *Butt-hole!*" I sang softly, and tried to sound a little like Darnell. "*Butt-hole! Butt-hole…*"

Mary laughed and giggled and then her leg seemed to get stuck on a stair. I reached to grab her but she fell forward too fast and I missed her and Mary fell like she had just learned how to dive except there was no water. She dived down the stairs with a thump and a smack and another thump. Mary didn't make a sound, but I heard one hard, hot, horrible breath from her, and then saw a swish and a splash of red as Mary's blood spilled down the stairs from her head and onto the floor, where it flowed like spilled smelly red milk.

I heard myself scream.

CHAPTER EIGHT

WHAT HAPPENED AFTER THAT WENT BY IN A WHIRL. I jumped down the stairs to try to hold Mary's head and stop all the blood from coming out. Conrad ran up, in his white pants, white coat, and shirt, and ripped off his coat, buttons popping, to wrap it around Mary. His coat was soaked red before I could blink my eyes.

Darnell and Tony ran down the stairs. Mrs. Byrne came running up to all of us, phone to her ear. She told Darnell, "Help me lift Mary's head, gently, and put it on my sweater." Then she lifted her blue sweater over her head, wrapped it in a ball, and put it under Mary's head.

"Yes, breathing," I heard Mrs. Byrne say into the phone. "But the eyes are flat."

The blood was like a lake. I felt sick. Mrs. Byrne told me, in a low voice, "Hold on to her hand, Sally. Squeeze Mary's hand."

I found Mary's fingers with mine and squeezed. I pressed the palm of my hand into her palm. I told Mary, "Mary, I love you. Mary, I'll help you. I'll do anything, Mary...."

Mary just gurgled. A man and a woman in blue uniforms ran up the stairs, looked into Mary's eyes, and put a mask over her nose and mouth. I heard a hiss of air. The man and woman mumbled numbers.

"I love you, Mary," I said again. "Don't leave, Mary."

The man and woman in blue took Mary down the stairs. Mrs. Byrne said that I couldn't come along, then put her arms around me and the next I knew we were in a taxicab.

All I could say was "I was in another cab just a few days ago."

The hospital was close. It was just next to the park. I told Mrs. Byrne, "Mary just fell. She didn't even trip. It was like..."

"I know, dear," said Mrs. Byrne.

We went up to the desk, where Mrs. Byrne talked to the people while I sat down. I saw a man in the waiting room with his hand wrapped in a shirt. I saw a woman asleep on her elbow. And I saw a man who held his sides and coughed so hard into his knees that I thought his head might come off. Some doors opened, and Conrad ran in—really, he ran in—and I saw that Mary's blood was spattered on his pants and shoes, too. But he had put a brown coat over his stained white shirt.

Conrad put his arms around me.

"Sal Gal. Sallie Gallie."

Then Conrad went over to Mrs. Byrne and put his arms around her, too. I was frightened, and Conrad turned around to me, smiled, and raised his thumb.

The man coughed into his knees again. The woman began to snore into her elbow.

"I didn't mean to hurt Mary," I said out loud, and began to cry. Conrad ran back, and then so did Mrs. Byrne. She put an arm around me.

"You didn't hurt Mary, Sally," she said. "Something went off in Mary's head. They call it a stroke, usually. That's why she fell. That's why she got hurt. All that—blood was from when she fell because of the stroke," she said softly. "You had nothing to do with what happened to Mary."

"You helped her with that scream, Sal Gal," said Conrad. "You helped by holding her hand."

But I still cried until my tears ran out and I felt them dry up on my face.

After a while, a doctor came out to the desk—she had a white mask pulled down over her throat and wore a light green coat and soft, squeaky shoes—and came over to where we sat when someone behind the desk pointed us out.

"You're here with Miss Gerrity?" she asked. "Mary Gerrity?"

Mrs. Byrne introduced us all, reaching over to squeeze my arm as she said my name and added, "Mary's very good friend. She was with her when—it happened."

"Ah. Well, I'm Dr. Ramasamy," said the doctor. "Mary is stabilized." I saw Mrs. Byrne sit back and let out a long breath. "She's had what we call a stroke. Blood was cut off in her brain. She's breathing fine now—pretty well, actually—and we'll just have to wait to see. To see how she is. Eventually."

"Can I see her?" I asked.

"Maybe tomorrow," said the doctor. "Or soon, anyway. She's resting now. We want to keep her that way. Rest and sleep may help Mary get better."

"We're in the same room," I told the doctor. "Mary rests better if I'm there." The doctor just made a kind face. So I asked, "When will she get better?"

"Well, she's better now," said the doctor. "Better than when she got here. But she's bleeding inside. That has to stop. She's swelling inside. Inside her head. That swelling has to go down. It takes time. There's no way to make it go quickly. Then we'll see how she is, Miss—?"

"Miyake," said Mrs. Byrne.

"Sal Gal," I told the doctor.

"I'm Pari," said the doctor with a slow smile. "A lot of people just can't get 'Ramasamy' out of their mouths. I answer to Sammy, too."

Dr. Sammy said she had to go back into the emergency room to help take care of Mary and other people who were sick.

"There's not much you can do for Mary out here,"

she told us. "You might want to go back to your Sunny-place."

"Sunnyside Plaza," I told her. "But what if Mary wakes up and I'm not here?"

Dr. Sammy looked at Mrs. Byrne and Mrs. Byrne looked at me.

"They'll call us. But really, it's best for Mary if she just sleeps."

"I can wait for her to wake up, can't I?"

"Conrad needs your help for lunch," said Mrs. Byrne.

"We'll be okay for lunch," said Conrad. "Darney, Tony, and Pilar."

"What if Mary needs my help?"

"That's why doctors and nurses are here," said Mrs. Byrne.

"But what if she needs me to hold her hand?" I said. "Like...like she did before..."

I felt myself crying again—long, hot drips and dribbles on my cheeks and chin. Dr. Ramasamy looked at all of us and said, "If you sit out here for a little while, Sal Gal, I'll come out now and then to keep an eye on you. Have you had breakfast?"

I shook my head no.

"I think we can get you some cereal."

"She likes Cheerios," Conrad told her.

"I'll stay a while longer, Sal," said Mrs. Byrne. "If you will."

A nice nurse brought me some Cheerios, and a glass of milk, while Conrad went back to Sunnyside Plaza, and Dr. Sammy went back through a door on the other side to take care of Mary, and I sat in the long room with the woman asleep on her arm and the man coughing into his knees, and lots of beeps and lights and voices crackling and gurgling numbers and names of doctors and nurses, and "Code Blue," or "Code Yellow," in the hard green hallways. The nurses watched me but were busy.

"I'm here, Mary," I murmured to myself. "Right here for you."

I waited for a while, ate my Cheerios, and watched people come and go. Mrs. Byrne called lots of people and talked in a low voice. Sometimes she got up and walked around to talk. There was a screen on all the time, right over our heads. I learned that there was a backup on the Stevenson. May cause flushing, headaches, and muscle pain. Where can you find the best pork jibarito sandwich? We'll hear from you! Calls from the IRS may be a scam! "Tom, I'm glad to see you, I'm worried about Ludmilla." "Ludmilla? But I saw her just yesterday...." The Board of Trade opened the same year as the Mexican-American War. Can anti-inflammatories treat Alzheimer's? We put the good in Good Morning! Use only as directed. Overnight temperatures will drop. Say bye-bye to wrinkles.

The doors whooshed open once again, and then Esther Rivas whooshed in, too.

She saw me in the chair, next to another chair with my empty bowl of Cheerios, and walked over in just a few long steps and leaned down to put her arms around my shoulders.

"Sal Gal," said Esther Rivas.

"Mary," I began, and started to cry again. It seemed that as soon as I ran out of tears, I'd save up some more, and then they'd overflow.

"I know," said Esther. She lifted up the empty bowl from the chair next to mine and sat down.

"I heard. You helped her. You, Darnell, Tony. Conrad. You—all of you—did good."

The bright lights got painful through the drops in my eyes, so I closed my eyes and put my head against Esther Rivas's shoulder. It was nice to smell roses and jasmine.

"I'm going to see the doctor here, Sally," she told me.

"Dr. Pari," I said.

"Maybe. Yes," said Esther. "Pari Ramasamy. You are always learning, aren't you, Sal Gal? Always paying attention. Taking things in, making notes. And that's why I want to ask you something. We—Detective Bridges and I—need your help."

I lifted my head from Esther's shoulder. Mrs. Byrne had come over.

"Laurence. Julius," Esther said. "They died. And now, Mary."

"She's not dead!" I said, and began to cry again. "Mary's not dead!"

Mrs. Byrne took hold of me, and Esther said, "No, she's not. Let's hope for the best. But you see, that's a lot to happen in Sunnyside Plaza in just a few weeks," said Esther. "One life lost—that happens. A second person—could be. But when Mrs. Byrne called us about Mary..."

Esther had problems speaking, too. She nodded at Mrs. Byrne.

"Well, that's just a lot." She was able to get it out finally. "And that's why we need you, Sal. You and your friends."

"I'll do anything to help Mary," I told her. "I'll do anything to help you."

"And Detective Bridges," Mrs. Byrne said as she smiled.

"Yes, maybe," I told Esther, and smiled back.

Esther leaned in even closer.

"I need you to think," she told me. "To look around Sunnyside. To try to remember. Anything. Anything unusual, or out of place. Or sometimes, things you look at every day, but don't really look at, because you look at them every day, and they don't seem unusual. So sometimes, you don't really see them. I need you and your friends to think about that, too. So we can figure out if something is going on at Sunnyside Plaza. If something there…"

Esther stopped and leaned in even a little closer.

"…someone there…or from outside who comes there…has done something that's not good. We have to find that out. We have to find that out soon. Sunny-side Plaza is a wonderful place, Sal Gal," Esther said. "But if these things happen and we can't find out why…"

Her voice ran out again, and it was a moment before Esther could find it to speak.

Mrs. Byrne had wet eyes, like a street after rain, and just said, "Well, the authorities will have to do something."

I didn't know that word.

"The city. The state. The police," Esther explained. "Sunnyside Plaza is a wonderful place, Sal. But if it's not safe for people…"

Esther Rivas's voice ran out again.

"My mother would have to come get me," I told her, and Mrs. Byrne squeezed my shoulder very tightly. She smiled again, straight into my eyes.

"Maybe," she said softly.

Esther stayed a little longer, but then Detective Bridges called and she had to leave. On the big, bright screen above, I saw a man get rid of dandruff, and a woman ride over a highway in a new red truck with a V8 engine. I watched a man melt marshmallows and milk chocolate over graham crackers in a red pot, and pop it all onto a plate with no mess, no fuss, and no messy cleanup, fast, fast, fast, like the pill you take for headaches and stomachaches. Works fast on tough stains. May cause constipation and nausea. Spicy, smooth, and satisfying.

CHAPTER NINE

SOMETIMES I WONDER: HAVE I MET MY MOTHER? I must have. I was in her stomach. She must have loved me. She must love me. But do I know her? I think of her sometimes. I hear a noise in the hall at night and think it might be her. I see a light across the window and think she must be coming. I know it's not. But something inside me jumps. I get ready. I close my eyes, so my mother will think I'm asleep and carry me away. Then I fall asleep, because my eyes are closed, and I think about that, and then I wake up. It's light out. My eyes are open. I see that it's the same world, dark or light. But I got through the night.

Conrad came to get me and I went back to Sunnyside Plaza. I looked around. I looked at everything. I looked at and counted the 8 times 4 squares of tile on the ceiling of my room, where the 2 times 8 plus 4 are cracked, and 2 times 8 plus 1 still have stains, and walked the 4 times 8 plus 4 stairs from the third floor to the first, calling each step by a number, and the 4 times 8 plus 4 stairs from the first floor to the third. Everything looked the same. Nothing looked wrong.

I went back into the kitchen and saw and counted all the pans, 2 times 8, and the pots, 8 plus 2, and 8 times 3 plus 4 chopping knives, and the 2 graters, and the 3 bowls with holes in the bottom where we plunk greens. I saw the 2 big cans of fruit to be fished on the counter, and the 7 big cans of fruit on the shelf over the refrigerator. I opened and closed the refrigerator. I saw 6 big cartons of milk, 2 big bottles of milk, 5 clumps of broccoli, 3 bags of short carrots, and a big square brick of butter. I counted 4 clear packs of ham and 6 clear packs of orange cheese slices and 1 clear pack of brown beef slices, and 2 bottles of ketchup and 1 bottle of mustard. I saw a package of crackers on the counter, the kind with salt on the top, that Conrad likes to eat and shares with us, and a big silver tub of flour, a tub of salt, a tub of sugar, and a tub where Conrad kept papers and coins and keys. Everything seemed fine. Everything was where it should be. There were 3 blocks of brown bread and 3 blocks of white bread (they tasted about the same, and sometimes Conrad would make me a special sandwich with brown on the bottom and white on the top, which made me giggle).

I went into the room where we ate and where we sometimes drew pictures and made cards. I counted 8 times 3 plus 5 white chairs that screeched when you pushed or pulled them, and 6 square tables and the calendar that showed a picture of a dog with a bow around his neck rubbing his wet nose on a yellow flower.

I walked the 4 times 8 plus 4 stairs from the first floor back to the third floor and lay down on my bed on the second floor and counted the 8 times 4 squares of tile on the ceiling, where the 2 times 8 plus 4 are cracked, and 2 times 8 plus 1 have stains, and tried to figure out what might be wrong at Sunnyside Plaza. What was different? What was wrong? What was out of place? What could go wrong if I didn't find out?

I closed my eyes and thought: Maybe if I fall asleep, my mother will come for me. Someday, I want a dog, I want to swim, I want to go to the North Pole, I want to wear something and smell like flowers. I want to go back to a baseball game.

CHAPTER TEN

I WENT DOWN TO HELP CONRAD FOR DINNER, BUT Tony and Darnell and Pilar had already helped and most everything was done. The kitchen smelled like soap and lemons. Conrad ran a towel over the counter, and I could hear people begin to walk in to get ready to sit down for dinner. We would have spaghetti with tomato sauce with a slice of bread and lettuce and green beans, and a big pan of yellow cake for dessert. I liked how the kitchen smelled, all tomatoes and garlic and hot oil and cake.

Conrad looked up and smiled.

"A long, tough day, Sal Gal. But you did good. You did great."

I smiled back.

"Let's hope our Mary Berry can be back with us," said Conrad. "Soon."

I came closer to speak softer.

"Conrad," I asked, "will they throw us out of Sunnyside Plaza?"

I could feel wet spots in my eyes again, and Conrad untied his apron and held an edge of it just below them.

"No," he told me. "No," he repeated. "*No*, Sallie Pallie. But we have to be practical. First off, much as we love Mary, after she's out of the hospital—well, Sunnyside might not be the best place for her. She may need some extra care that we can't give her."

"I'll do anything to care for Mary. I'll feed her, I'll dress her, I'll—"

"I know that, Sal," said Conrad. "I truly do, and so does she. But sometimes, much as we love them, well…sometimes, we just aren't the best people to be able to help the people we love. Maybe," Conrad said, even more soft than ever, "that's what your momma

119

decided when you were a bitty baby. Maybe she felt like she didn't know what to do, or how to begin, to help you. Besides...well, if something is wrong here...if there's something here that's not good for people..."

"Where will we go?" I asked Conrad. I could feel myself shake, and it wasn't cold. "What will we do? Will my mother come?"

Conrad put his hands on my shoulders, and it made me shake a little less.

"Sal Gal, I don't know any of that. But I won't let anything bad happen to you. Do you hear me? Do you know that?"

Conrad looked into my eyes—we were the same height—and I nodded, up and down.

"I'll do whatever I have to for you. For Darney, for Pilar, for Tony." Conrad turned back to the counter, and the towel, but kept talking to me.

"I never met people like you before I got here," he said. "And I think God puts certain people right in front of you because you're supposed to help each other. You've sure helped me."

I had stopped crying and was starting to laugh a little.

"I've helped you, Conrad?"

"Every day."

He crossed his heart and held up a finger toward the sky.

"Chopping, wiping. Pear fishing?" I asked.

Conrad put an arm around my shoulders and told me, "That and some other stuff, Sal Gal."

The spaghetti was good and Tony mixed in his lettuce, so most of the rest of us did, too, and that made it crunch. I used the bread like a sponge, and when I plopped my plate into the garbage can, Pilar said, "It's so clean, like my dog licked it." Pilar wants a dog, too, like me. The yellow cake had brown frosting. Tony said it was chocolate, Shaaran said no, it was peanut. I couldn't tell, and didn't really care, and ate it in 4 bites.

Matt, Keesha, and Vy didn't eat dinner but ate their cake. Jimmy said "birdie" when he finished his spaghetti, and then once before he didn't eat his cake. I looked around for something wrong but saw nothing.

Pilar and Darnell and me went back to the kitchen

to help Conrad put things away. Darnell almost always lifts up the big cans, because he's so big, and he put one of the big cans of tomatoes against his big belly and began to lift and then stopped when a label that wrapped around the can got loose and stuck over his thumb.

"The can bites," Darnell said, but he laughed as he said it and shook his thumb like it was on fire.

"Labels slip sometimes," said Conrad, "with all the handling, heat, and steam." And he reached over and began to wrap the label into a ball. A smaller label fell out of the ball and fell flat on the counter. Conrad picked up the label and squinted. Then he reached into his pocket, took out a pair of glasses, put them up to his eyes, and squinted again. He unrolled the ball he'd made from the label and smoothed it out on top of the counter.

"That SOB," he said softly. I knew the word was bad, but didn't know why, and I burst out with a short laugh before I could stop.

"George," Conrad explained. "George Nellos. The guy who delivers canned goods here. Gives us a good price, too, he says. But it looks like he gave us some old, outdated stuff here."

Conrad pointed a finger to a jumble of numbers on the label he'd unwrinkled.

"See?" he said. "It's all here after it says 'Sell by...' and the numbers that follow."

"Like a story," I said. "Like the big board at the ballpark."

"Exactly, Sallie Gallie," he said. "And the story here is that the numbers say this is a can that should have been used six years ago. Sheesh."

"Sheesh," Darnell repeated. "Sounds like a bad word, too."

"It's close to one," Conrad agreed. "Let's take a look at this one of apple slices," he said, and put the can down on its side and rolled it over until he found the edge of the label and began to lift it off with his thumb.

Conrad held up his glasses and squinted again.

"This one expired seven years ago. George, that SOB," Conrad repeated.

"Is that like 'butthole'?" Darnell asked him. "A word we shouldn't say?"

"Only say it when no other word will do, Darney," he told him. "And I'm beginning to think maybe we should. Do me a favor, my friend, and bring that little ladder over here."

Darnell picked up the small white stepladder and opened it in front of the counter. Conrad stepped up 1, 2, 3 stairs, and picked up one of the big cans, and handed it down to Darnell, who handed it to me, then another one to Pilar. We put them both on the counter. Then Conrad handed another can to Darnell, who handed it to me, then another down to Pilar.

Conrad came down from the ladder and began to run his thumb under a label, then another, then another.

"Tomatoes," he said out loud. "Six, seven years old. The pears here—eight years old. Peaches—five years old. These apples—seven years old. Son of a—"

"You shouldn't say it, Conrad," said Darnell. "If you say it, I'll say it."

What Conrad finally said to finish his words was "Son of a...female dog, pardon my French. All of these cans. What a scam. Butthole!"

"Butthole!" Darnell repeated, and Conrad just laughed and didn't tell him he shouldn't talk like that.

"George delivers tomorrow," Conrad said. "George and I are going to have a little conversation. We're gonna put these cans over by the garbage—'cause that's where they belong—and tomorrow George and I are gonna have a little conversation."

We were all laughing by the time we turned the corner, and Conrad left to go home, and Darnell and Pilar and I went upstairs, and we all smiled to see Jimmy sitting in the corner of the room where people watched whatever was on the screen and to hear him say "birdie" when we walked by. Bad things had happened all around us, but we knew each other and were happy.

I closed the door to our room and lay down on the top of my bed and looked up at the 8 times 4 squares of tile on the ceiling—2 times 8 plus 4 are still cracked, and 2 times 8 plus 1 of them still have brown stains. I looked at the ceiling and tried to remember what I'd heard Esther Rivas and Lon Bridges say to Mrs. Byrne, and what Mrs. Byrne said to them.

I know I'm *different*. That's how people say it, so they think you won't know what they mean. But I do. I know we're *different*—Mary, Tony, Pilar, Darnell, Shaaran, Ray, Jimmy, all of us at Sunnyside Plaza. I know we're *different* because of the way a lot of people on the outside look at us when they come in here. The way they talk to us. Or talk like we're not here. Like we can't hear them. Or if we do, so what? We're not people like they are, they think. We're *different*.

I know lots of things go into my mind. Cows have 4 stomachs. There's a town called Bacon, Texas. The moon isn't really made of green cheese. Mrs. Byrne has a husband named Tim and a son named Jace. Stepladders, $79.99 at Home Depot! Violin and fiddle—they're the same thing. There are 5 kinds of hurricanes. Oxygen action helps shrink swelling. It's 7 to 2 in the fourth. Tractor-trailer overturned, backup on the Bishop Ford. More than half the people in the world have brown eyes. I do. But I guess I don't always have a shelf in my head where I can put the things that come into my mind, keep them in place, and get them when I need them.

I knew I needed to put things into place now.

I looked up at the ceiling and counted the 8 times 4 squares of tile and then sat up, got up, opened the door, and called out into the hall.

CHAPTER ELEVEN

Tony, Darnell, and Pilar all watched some kind of game in the big room, but mostly to see the messages when the game wasn't going on. Smooth and satisfying. Better mileage. Do you suffer from irritable bowel syndrome? Extra-crunchy. May cause flu-like symptoms.

But they stood up so that we could stand in the hall and talk. Whisper, really.

"Something is wrong here," I told them, but not too loud.

"I'll say," said Darnell, who was louder.

But Tony asked, "What's wrong?"

"All the people who get sick," I told them.

"Who's sick?" said Tony.

"Laurence," Darnell reminded him.

"Laurence died," Pilar remembered, and Darnell made a face like something spilled.

"That's really sick," he said.

"And Julius," I reminded them.

"One, two," said Tony.

"And remember Stevie," I told them.

Tony did.

"The old girl with a boy's name," he said.

"She was short," Pilar remembered.

"She went somewhere," said Darnell.

"They said she was sick," Tony recalled.

"Sick, and then we never saw her again," I told them.

Then Darnell remembered something—or someone else.

"Julie-ahna. Julie-anna. Or something."

"She went away, too," said Tony. "They never said she was sick."

"I was around the corner from the kitchen and heard Esther and Lon," I said.

"Our friends," said Darnell.

"Yes. Our friends," I said, and dropped my voice

real low and got closer than ever to Tony, Pilar, and Darnell.

"Esther and Lon," I told them. "I heard them say old food can hurt people if they take pills."

Tony asked, "Old food?"

"I eat food," said Darnell. "Food doesn't get old with me."

"I take pills," Pilar said.

"We all do," Tony pointed out.

"We all do," I agreed. "Conrad read the labels on cans of food. In the kitchen."

"Apples and peaches?" asked Pilar. "Pears?"

"Anything," I told them. "Everything. The man who brings us the cans put new labels on old cans. Conrad saw that they'd put bad labels on old cans. The food inside was old. Conrad was mad—almost as mad as I've seen. He put the cans next to the garbage. He said that's where they should be. But Conrad didn't hear Esther and Lon. He didn't hear them talk about how old food can make us sick."

"If we take pills," said Pilar.

"We all take pills," said Darnell.

"We have to tell someone," said Tony. "Not just each other."

"Someone who can do something," I agreed, and then paused. "Esther. Lon."

"They won't believe us," said Tony. "No one outside believes us. You see that. You know what I mean. People come in here and smile at us. Then they laugh at us. Or get scared of us. Or say we're sweet. Or make fun of us. They don't believe us."

I held out one of the labels and said, "They have to believe us. They see this, they have to believe us. What they need to know—it's right here. Esther and Lon can see that."

"That's just paper," said Darnell. "Itty-bitty paper. Anyone can put anything on paper. We have to show them cans."

"The cans are on the shelf in the kitchen," said Pilar. "I can't reach them."

"I can," said Darnell. "On the little ladder."

"But we can't take any cans," Pilar pointed out.

"We won't open them or eat them," I told her. "We'll just show them to Lon and Esther. Tonight."

"Tonight?" said Darnell. His voice got louder. "I go to bed at night."

"Before we brush our teeth and go to bed," I told everyone. "Esther says quick. Soon. Because if something is wrong here, we might not be able to stay."

Everyone looked at each other, then everyone looked at the floor, then everyone looked back at each other.

"My mother would get me," Pilar said finally. "Maybe. If she could. If she could, I'm sure she'd come get me. If she knew."

There was a long silence before Darnell said, "My momma would come get you. And me too. If she knew. She'd come get all of us. But I don't know who cares about us. We got to get some of those cans," he said.

"They close the kitchen. At night. It's locked now," said Pilar.

"Dorothy locks the kitchen," Tony agreed. "We can't get any cans."

"Dorothy locks the kitchen," I said. "But Conrad hides a key."

Everyone looked at me. They waited for me to say something more.

"Above the door. I know where, I think. Conrad always says, 'What if Dorothy gets stuck in snow? What if Dorothy is sick? What if she just forgets?' "

"What if we go downstairs," said Darnell, "and see what we can do."

We left everyone in the big room, watching and watching. We heard voices boom from the room down the hall. Fresh new look, same great taste! You can't beat our prices. We must be crazy! Fights gingivitis. Adds bounce and shine.

"We sure must be crazy," Darnell whispered as we stepped softly down the 4 times 8 plus 4 steps to the bottom floor and the kitchen.

"Look up there," I told everyone. "Count 4 tiles over from the corner."

"I don't count," Darnell said.

"One, two, three, four," said Tony. "So?"

"I've seen Conrad put a key up there. On that steel shelf."

Pilar pulled over a chair. Darnell said, "Guess you want me to do something, don't you?" He chuckled and took 1, 2 steps up, put a hand against the white tiles of the wall, and the other on top of the shelf.

"I feel nothing," he told us.

132

"Move your hand over," Tony told him. "Toward the doorway."

Darnell did and told us, "Nothing."

"Now back the other way," I told him, and we heard a scuff and a scrape and then Darnell said, "Ouch." He turned and smiled down at us.

"Caught a key," he told us.

Darnell came down from the chair and held out his hand. There was a gold key on a chain with a small pink pig and red marks or letters on it that I didn't know.

"I love that pig!" said Pilar.

"The pig is cute," said Tony. "But I don't know what to do with a key."

"People tap numbers to open doors," said Pilar.

"There aren't numbers on our doors," said Tony. "Or keys. I don't know about keys."

What did any of us know about keys? We didn't use keys. We didn't carry keys. There were no locks on our doors to open or close. Keys were only in the world out there, where people kept things behind doors.

I asked everyone, "Did you ever use a key?"

No one answered.

"I've seen it," said Darnell. "Plenty of times. You stick it in the handle like..."

Darnell poked the key in the handle 1, 2, 3 times and stopped.

"It doesn't go."

Tony bent down and looked at the handle, with 1 eye very close.

"The hole is small. Give it here."

Tony pushed the key into the handle 1 time, 2 times, and then we heard an iron crunch.

"Got it!" he said. "What now?"

"You push, you pull, you jiggle the key up and down," said Darnell. He put his hand on the fat end of the key and pushed. Then he pulled. Then he jiggled up and down.

We all laughed, but after I laughed, I told them, "Quiet. We don't want Dorothy or anyone to hear us."

Then we all got quiet. But Pilar whispered loudly, "You don't open a door just by wiggling your butt-butt," and we all made coughing sounds when we tried to stop from laughing.

Darnell wiggled the key back and forth again and pushed with his shoulder into the door.

He grunted.

"Dorothy must be really strong," he said. "Stronger than me."

Darnell groaned and grunted and wiggled his butt-butt again.

"I'll try," said Pilar.

She put a hand on the knob and the other on the key and wiggled it a little, but just a little.

"Let me try," I said, and wiggled the key and leaned against the door with my shoulder.

We heard a click. I turned the knob in Pilar's hand, and the door groaned. Pilar took a step back, and then the door squeaked and scraped along the floor as it slid back slowly with a new groan and we saw lights from the street through a window shine on pots and pans and in our eyes. It was dark, but we were in the kitchen.

"Quick," I told everyone. "Quiet. So no one hears us."

Tony dragged the small ladder over to the kitchen counter and Darnell took 1, 2, 3 steps up the ladder. He put a hand on Tony's shoulder.

"Got a can of pears here," he said, and handed it

down to Pilar. "Apples," he said then, and held out the can. I took it from his hand and held it to my chest.

"Tomatoes, too," said Tony, and Darnell told him, "I get these. Something orange here, too."

"Oranges?" asked Pilar. "We don't get oranges."

"Maybe it's pumpkin," I told them. "You know— Christmas."

"Peaches," said Darnell. "Got to be peaches." He handed down another can, and I told everyone, "We've got what we need."

We closed the door. Pilar locked it—quickly. Tony had his hands on a can of pears, Darnell had a can of tomatoes in his arms, I had apples, and Pilar had peaches. We all wondered, but didn't have to ask, "What do we do now?"

I told everyone, "We have to get these cans to Esther and Lon."

"They're at the police station," Darnell said.

"Yes. There," I told him. "We have to get them there. Now."

"Where is that?" asked Tony.

"It's close. I know that," I said. "It's also near the

ballpark. It's near the ballpark that's near here, so it's near here."

"There's a lot near here," said Pilar. "It's the city. But how do we get there?"

"We walk," I said, and we all stopped a moment to look at each other in the dark of the hallway.

"You mean...out there?" asked Tony.

"We don't go out there," said Pilar. "Not by ourselves."

"We have to now," I told them. "If we're going to get these to Esther and Lon in time."

We all stood and looked at each other. Then Darnell started to walk through the dark hallway to the front door of Sunnyside Plaza, and Pilar went behind him, and then Tony.

And then me.

We looked at the back of the front door. It was bright yellow, with big chips of paint chipped off, so there were also chips of brown, and there was the eyehole in the center, as high as an eye. Dorothy and Mrs. Byrne sometimes let us look through the eyehole to see the chins of people who rang to get in, or to see people walk by on the street.

And there was a lock.

"It's locked," said Pilar. "We can't get out."

"Sure we can," Darnell told us. "Here's what Dorothy does."

Darnell put his hand on a small knob and turned it. We heard a pop and a click and the door opened a crack.

Darnell turned around and smiled.

"I watched her," he said.

Pilar took a step and stood in front of the door.

"I didn't know," she said. "I didn't know it was so easy."

"The lock is easy," Darnell told her. "Walking out into out there—that's not easy."

Darnell pulled back on the door. The sounds of feet and buses and voices began to float in, and we knew that if we were ever going to walk out, we would have to walk out before all the sounds could float upstairs.

We all took the first step more or less at the same time. We saw a bus go by, with bright white lights inside and people sleeping, reading, and looking out the window. There were blinking red lights next door, and yellow lights across the street, and silver streetlights above us, and buildings to the sky, and people hurrying by, and above all that were silver-white clouds, and twinkle-twinkle silver stars, and a silver moon that spilled light on our hands and faces. We were all by ourselves in the world outside.

I was scared. I was excited. I took a step.

And then another. I was so excited, I stopped counting steps.

CHAPTER TWELVE

IT WAS JUST A FEW STEPS BEFORE TONY TOLD US, "We're lost. Already."

"We're not lost," said Darnell. "We don't know where we're going."

"We know where we're going," said Pilar. "We don't know how to get there."

There was a big window with large red letters that looked like they were on fire. There were people inside, but they didn't sit together, and they looked out the window and into a mirror over what they drank. There were glasses stacked on top of each other and faucets that spit suds into glasses.

"They might know," I said, and we pushed in the door. We heard a few soft voices and sad music. A man with a ponytail behind his head who stood behind a tall counter asked, "Beer?"

Darnell asked, "What?"

"Can I get you a beer?" asked the man.

"A what?" asked Darnell, and the man behind the counter made a face and laughed.

"Okay. I get it. You're not a beer guy—just top-shelf scotch, am I right?"

"I can reach the top shelf," Darnell told the man.

"Can you tell us how to get to the police station?" I asked, and a man who sat on a stool a little space away turned around to say, "Darling, the police usually find me."

A woman in black pants and a black apron and a white shirt and bright red hair came over and stood in front of that man. She looked at us with a smile but told the man behind the counter, "Nicky, I think these folks may be from the home over there."

She tugged her shoulder toward a wall.

"Oh," said the man who had the name Nicky. "Oh, right, over there. Sunnydale."

"Sunnyside Plaza," I told him.

He asked, "You work with Bob and Dorothy?"

"We know them," said Tony. "Sure."

"But I think," said the lady with red hair, "that they're—"

She pulled on her shoulder again.

"You live there?" asked Nicky. "Or work there?"

"Oh, both," Pilar told him. "We work in the kitchen."

"With those funny people?"

"Nicky!" the woman almost yelled, and Nicky started to flap his lips before he could speak.

"Oh, shoot," he said. "I see. I don't mean anything. Have a drink."

"Nicky!" the woman cried again.

"Well, I bet they could use one," he said.

"Orange juice, Nicky," she said. "On me. On *you*, for what you said."

Nicky pointed a finger at the can Darnell had under his arm.

"Looks like our friends brought their own."

Darnell laughed and said, "That's tomatoes."

"We each have a different can," Pilar told Nicky. "Peaches, apples, pears."

"You afraid of running out?"

Darnell laughed again.

"We have a counter, too," he told him. "In our kitchen. At Sunnyside. Our kitchen smells nicer."

Nicky lifted up a carton of orange juice from behind his counter and began to pour the juice into a glass.

"Is it old?" Darnell asked him.

"Old?" asked Nicky. "Old juice?"

"You can see on the label," I told Nicky. "There are numbers."

Nicky lifted the carton up above his nose and looked hard.

"It says here the oranges in this juice were picked just two days ago by elves in little green suits."

Pilar said, "Wow."

The woman with red hair and black pants yelled out "Nicky!" again.

The man on the stool turned around again, and said "wow," too.

"I think it's a joke," I told Pilar. "Isn't it?" I asked Nicky.

The woman with red hair leaned over the counter and took her own look at the carton.

"The label says sell by the end of the week," she told us. "It's fine."

"We have to be careful," I told her. "We take pills."

"Oh, so do I," said the lady. "Aspirin, blood pressure. I'm Jackie," she told me. "Why are you looking for the police station?"

Nicky poured out 1, 2, 3, 4 glasses of orange juice and handed them to Darnell, Pilar, Tony, and me.

"We need their help. We need to show them something."

"Can I help?" asked Jackie. "We can call the police. You usually call the police when you need them to help."

"Thank you," I said, and took a sip of orange juice. "But we have to see some people there—Esther Rivas and London Bridges—who told me to look around for something, and I did."

Darnell drank his orange juice as he listened and then told Jackie, "People don't hear us, sometimes. People think we don't know things, so they don't hear us. We have to show them if we want them to hear us."

Jackie seemed to think about that and said, "I hear you. Well, the police station is one block up, two blocks over."

"Up?" I asked. "In the sky?"

The man on the stool laughed.

"You're funny. Really funny. What's your name?"

"What's that to you, Marvin?" Jackie asked him.

"Sally," I told them. "Sal Gal."

"Well, Sally Sal Gal," said Jackie, " 'up' in this case means you go out our door and go left. For a block." She looked at her wrist. "Then you turn right."

"Right?" I asked, and Jackie lightly tapped one of my shoulders.

"This side," she told me. "You can tell a block is over when you see a new street. You'll see that after you go left"—and Jackie tapped my other shoulder— "and get to the corner. There's a church mission there."

Jackie must have seen my face and knew that I didn't know what she meant, really.

"Like a church. But it doesn't look like a church. It's a big, lighted room where people sing and pray." Jackie tapped Marvin on the top of his head. "They pray for Marv."

Marvin turned around to say, "I don't need prayers."

"You don't need another beer," Jackie told him. "That's what you really don't need." And then she turned back to me. "The mission has prayer and song meetings. They should have one tonight. They're not police. But they try to help people. Maybe you could stop there and ask them to point you toward the police station. You sure I can't call your friends there? Esther and—is that really his name? London Bridges?"

I nodded my head.

"It sure is," I told her. "But we have to show them the cans so they'll know."

Jackie leaned a little closer to me.

"Is it...safe for you to be out...here?" she asked.

"It's...different," I told her. "We don't go out much."

"Are you okay?"

"Oh yes," I said.

"Should I...call someone?"

"Oh no. Our police friends are detectives. We have to find them, show them, and they'll help," I told Jackie. "I'm sure."

"Well, we're here," she said. "If you find your way back." Then Jackie, the red-haired lady, took hold of my hands.

"A lot of people come in here looking for something, Sal Gal," she said. "At the bottom of a glass. And they just try glass after glass, and never find what they want. But I think you're looking at life the right way, Sal Gal. You're on your way."

Nicky was pouring more orange juice into everyone's glass, but I told them all, "We better go."

Marvin put his hand over his glass and told Nicky, "Don't let orange juice break my beer glass." A couple of other people in the back of the place laughed, and as Darnell opened the door for the rest of us, we saw the red sign on fire again, and Darnell said to us, "That was good, wasn't it? I like it out here."

CHAPTER THIRTEEN

THE PLACE THAT JACKIE, THE RED-HAIRED LADY, told us to look for was not far away. It looked as bright as she said, with large windows that shined yellow light onto the street. We saw shadows on the sidewalk, and then saw that they were our shadows.

Tony pretended that his shadow bopped Darnell's shadow. Pilar pretended that her shadow bit my shadow like a shark. I pretended that my shadow was a huge giant in the sky.

We saw a couple of the people inside the place, and they began to look at us, so we walked in. There were a few people, 1, 2, 3, 4, 5, 6 in folding chairs, who looked like they were sleeping, or trying to sleep, or just closed their eyes, and 1 of the men in a chair blinked his eyes when his chin fell on his chest. Then he opened his eyes big, like baseballs, and he shouted, "Praise!" and closed his eyes again.

"Shouts like Jimmy," said Darnell.

We smelled coffee, candles, and a bathroom.

There was a man in a white shirt and a skinny black tie and shiny black shoes, who came across the room to us.

"Your hair is shiny," Pilar told him.

The man took a half step back before he told us, "Well, thanks. No one has said that before. Thanks, I guess. I'm Pastor Chuck. Can I offer you some coffee?"

"I know coffee," I told him.

"It's late to see coffee," Tony told him.

Pastor Chuck held a finger to his lips and turned toward 3 people in the back part of the room. They were standing. They sang:

Come, thou almighty King,
help us thy name to sing,
help us to praise!

The man in the chair blinked once more and cried out, "Praise!"

"Isn't that beautiful?" asked Pastor Chuck. "Don't they sing so beautifully?"

"They sure sing beautiful," Darnell told him. "My momma sings to me like that."

"They're students at the bible institute. Welcome to you, brothers and sisters," said Pastor Chuck. "I'm so glad you were led into our midst tonight."

"I don't think we're brothers and sisters," I told him.

"Darnell sure is not my brother," Pilar added. "Eeeew…"

Tony looked around and said, "I have a brother. At home. Is he here?"

"You are all our brothers and sisters," said Pastor Chuck. "Have you accepted your Lord and Savior?"

We looked at each other, until finally I said, "I'm not sure."

"We can hear your declaration right now," said Pastor Chuck. "That way, you can know that whatever happens, you're in God's loving arms."

A woman came over to us and smiled. She had on blue pants and a white shirt and short yellow hair.

"Chuck, I think maybe they're here for something else. I'm Pastor Liz—Mary Elizabeth," she told us, and shook each of our hands and said, "Blessings to you," each time.

"Ah-choo!" said Darnell. "Ah-choo to you!"

"I like your humor," said Pastor Liz. "We could all use more humor, couldn't we? Do you carry those cans everywhere?" she asked us.

Tony looked down at his can of pears, Darnell looked down at his tomatoes, Pilar looked down at her peaches, and I hugged my can of apples to my chest.

"Just for now. We have to show them to the police. That's why we're out here."

Pastor Liz thought about that for a moment and just said, "Well. I see. Of course. And how can we help?" she asked us.

I told Pastor Liz, "We're trying to find where the police are."

"Oh. The police station, I'll bet. You're close. Just a few blocks up. But is there something…special… about those cans? The police are mighty busy. Maybe I can help."

"The cans are old," I told Pastor Liz. "The stuff inside is old. It's not good for us. We take pills."

"May I…see?" asked Pastor Liz. I looked at

Darnell, and he looked at Tony, who looked at Pilar, who looked back at me, and finally I said, "Sure."

I held up my can of apples and put a finger on the label.

"The story is in those numbers," I told her, and Pastor Liz scrunched down her eyes to read.

"It looks okay," she said slowly. "Just last year... but wait... I see."

She unscrunched her eyes and looked straight at me.

"It's a new label, isn't it? Over an old label. Should we take it off and see?"

Pilar and Darnell and Tony and I looked back and forth at each other and thought.

"Just a little ways," Pastor Liz then suggested. "Just to see if there's something to see."

We thought some more and then I told Pastor Liz, "Okay. Just a little."

I held on to the can of apples, and Pastor Liz ran her fingernail under the corner of the label, and we heard just a light crackle.

Then Pastor Liz smiled, but she said, "Oh no." Then she said, "You're right." Then she said, "This can of apples expired six years ago."

"Conrad says the man who sold it to us is an SOB," said Darnell. I didn't think that was a word you should say, but Pastor Liz just smiled.

"Everyone is a child of God," she said. "But yes, some children of God can be SOBs, too."

"Or buttholes," said Darnell, and Pastor Liz smiled again as she said, "That's not how I'd put it. But every soul is different. So you're trying to get to the police?"

"We got here by walking up," I told her. "From the place with red fire in the window."

"Sounds like Ollie's," said Pastor Chuck. "Ollie's Lodge. We get a lot of people in here after they've been to Ollie's."

"Marv?" asked Tony.

"I don't know if we know him," said Pastor Chuck. "Some folks don't tell us their real name. But chances are, we'll see Marv someday."

There was another man who came up behind Pastor Liz and whispered something. She nodded yes to him, then cleared her throat and told him, "Give us just a few moments longer, brother. We'd be pretty poor pastors if we didn't hold off our praise of God for just a few minutes, so we can do a little of God's work."

"We're about to begin our worship," Pastor Chuck told us. "Do you all have faith?"

We looked at each other again.

"Belief," Pastor Chuck explained. "Belief in something larger." And after a moment or so, Darnell slapped his belly and laughed.

"This is larger," Darnell said, and Pastor Chuck and Pastor Liz laughed, too.

"You're welcome to join us," she said. "But I know you're eager to be on your way. You're from one of the homes near here?"

"Sunnyside Plaza," I told her. "That's our home."

"I've got a home and a mother, too," said Pilar. "And a dog and a cat and a swing and a brother."

"You're so lucky," Pastor Liz told Pilar, and then turned slightly to me to say, "And Sunnyside Plaza sounds like a lovely place. Do you have fun there?"

"Oh yes. We all work in the kitchen," I told her. "We draw. We watch things. I went to a baseball game."

"I drew a bird," Pilar told her, too. "I used every color on the table."

"That sounds beautiful, too," said Pastor Liz. "What you have to do after you go out of here," she went on, "is to keep going. One block, then two blocks. You'll see a place called Peking Duke's. They have a little red pig all lit up in their window."

"I just saw a little red pig!" Darnell was excited. "On a chain on a key! Tonight!"

"Well, you'll know it when you see it, then," said Pastor Liz. "And right across the street, a little ways down, you'll see the police station. Should I ask one of the students here to go with you?"

"They have to sing," I told her.

"May Pastor Chuck and I send you off with a prayer?" asked Pastor Liz. "We believe prayers help. Especially when nothing else does."

Darnell, Pilar, and Tony and I looked at each other back and forth until Tony said, "Yes. Sure. But I don't know any prayers."

"Pastor Chuck and I know enough for all of us," said Pastor Liz. "But meeting you folks has been like seeing prayers in front of us. It must take courage to go out into a world you don't know very well," she said. "To find the strength to do something that might frighten you. But I see how you give each other strength to take step after step."

Pastor Liz and Pastor Chuck held their hands over our heads and bowed their heads and closed their eyes. When Pastor Liz began to speak, I closed my eyes, too.

"Lord, thank you for sending these friends into our midst," she said. "They share your good news with every step. Please hold them in your hand on their journey."

"Ayyy-men!" said Darnell. "Did I do that right?"

The man in the folding chair shouted, "Praise!" then closed his eyes.

We went out of the door, laughing, and into the street. Another bus rolled by and people hurried by the big window, and our laughs bounced off the glass and into the street, where we could hear the bible students begin to sing, *Throw out the lifeline across the dark wave, there is a brother out there whom someone should save,* before the door closed behind us and we took our next steps up the street, through all the sounds of walking and talking and sirens.

CHAPTER FOURTEEN

WE KEPT ON GOING—1 STEP BY 1 STEP, ALL OF US. WE walked, and we looked. Bricks were red, brown, and even gray. Windows were wide, small, and tall. Sidewalks were gray, flat, and cracked. People looked at us, and they looked away. We saw twigs on the street, old stains, and little crushed leaves. We saw people in windows sipping, thinking, talking, and dreaming. And then Tony said, "I see a red pig."

It was ahead of us, across a street. A bright red pig, big as a person, on the front of a building over a street across the way. We held on to our cans in our arms, and waited for a light to turn green and cars to stop and hold up, and ran across. I heard all our feet scuff over the street.

"That's my red pig," said Darnell. "Big and bright."

The big red pig glowed over a big red door. Tony pushed it open and we followed. A young-looking man smiled and asked, "One, two, three, do I see four?"

"Yes," I told him. "I guess so."

I looked around and saw people eating and realized that it was a place to eat. I wasn't sure what we should do.

"We need directions," I told the man.

"We can help," he said. "But wouldn't you like a snack first?" Then he held out a hand so we could see a bright yellow round couch around a round table.

"There are flowers on the couch," said Pilar.

"Wow, there are," said the man. "All this time, I never noticed. What would you like to eat?"

"We get to eat?" asked Darnell.

"Everybody has to eat," the man told us. "That's why we're here."

"A ham sandwich," said Tony, and the rest of us added "me too," one right after another.

"No ham," the young man told us. "No sandwiches. We have pork. Pork buns, barbecue pork, ginger and pork noodle soup, pork fried rice, moo shoo pork. Pork egg rolls."

"Egg rolls sounds funny," said Pilar.

"Eggs roll, eggs break," said Darnell.

"They don't roll," the man explained. "And there's no egg in them. Maybe a little in the dough. You don't know Chinese food?"

"Don't they eat it in China?" I asked.

"They eat it everywhere," he said. "All over the world. For a long time. They eat Chinese food here, they eat it in Mexico, they eat it in Indiana. I bet they even have Chinese food at the North Pole."

"I want to go to the North Pole!" I told him.

"Have the egg rolls there," he told us with a smile. "Then tell me if ours aren't better. My grandfather started this restaurant."

Tony told him, "My grandfather has a scratchy chin. He scrapes everybody when he kisses them. That's what my mother says."

"Hey, mine too," the man told us. "We used to say, 'Hey, Grandpa, just blow us a kiss.' Hey, egg rolls are a good start for you. I'll bring eight."

"That's 2 for you, 2 for you, 2 for you, 2 for me," I told everyone.

"The orange sauce there is sweet," said the man, pointing to a bowl in the middle of the table with 2 sauces and 2 colors. "The yellow sauce is spicy—be careful."

As soon as the man turned around and walked away, Darnell put a small finger in the orange sauce and licked it.

"Mighty sweet," he told us. "You'll like it."

"What about the yellow?" Tony asked.

Darnell told us, "I'm not gonna try something when someone says, 'Be careful.'"

The man brought the food to us and 1, 2, 3, 4 small plates. The food—the egg rolls—looked like big fat golden puffy fingers, not rolls. They smelled delicious.

There were forks, knives, and spoons already on the table, and red napkins and a red envelope that Pilar tore open with her teeth. It had 2 small sticks inside.

"I've seen those," said Tony. "You stab food with them," he said, and took a stick and tried to stab one of the egg rolls. But the egg roll rolled away. Pilar had to stop it with her knuckles, before it rolled off the plate.

"Egg rolls roll!" she said.

We left the sticks next to the plates and picked up forks. Darnell held his egg roll like a Popsicle and took a bite. Then we all did. I could taste onions and green things and crispy stuff. We plopped down the sweet sauce, and dragged our egg rolls through the orange pool, and took more bites.

"Can Conrad do these for us sometime?" asked Pilar.

"Like, every time," said Darnell.

There were 1, 2, 3, 4, 5, 6 more people in the place, also eating. They lifted their heads, looked at us, and looked away. A man laughed. A woman got up and left, in a hurry. Another woman called over the young man and whispered something. She frowned. She whispered, but she looked angry.

The nice man came back to us and made sure we had water, then asked if we'd like tea.

"Tea," said Pilar. "Dorothy has tea sometimes. She puts a little bag in water."

The man made a face and shook his shoulders.

"Not at Peking Duke's," he told us. "Never. Tea leaves have to breathe. I'll show you."

He brought over a small red pot and lifted the lid. A little cloud came out.

"Take a whiff," he said. We did.

"Flowers," I said. "And oranges."

The man poured out hot tea into small cups for all of us. Darnell picked up his cup in his hands.

"It's hot," he said. "Like hot chocolate."

Pilar took a small sip.

"But it's just hot," she said. "Not chocolate."

Tony blew on the cloud coming out of his cup.

"My cloud is going to rain on Darnell," he said. "Darnell is gonna get wet."

Darnell took a sip of tea and made a face.

"Tastes like oranges a little, Sal Gal," he told me. "But mostly it tastes like a tree."

"Tea," Pilar said to him, but Darnell just repeated:

"Tree. *Tree*. Tea tastes like *tree*."

We were all laughing and sipping and making faces and laughing when we heard a siren down the street and saw a big blue light blinking off of the mirrors on the walls of the place we were eating, and the lady who had whispered and frowned was standing up in her blue coat and shaking and pointing at us.

"I called!" she shouted. "I told them crazy people are in here!" Her voice trembled. "What is this world coming to when you go out for dinner and have to look at all these strange, scary, crazy people!"

"Who? What?" asked Darnell, and the woman's yell got so loud it made our ears hurt and turn red. I could see people in the eating place begin to stand and look around or sit low in their seats.

"Get out!" the woman shouted at us. "Now!"

The big red door swung open and the big blue blinking light filled the room. I heard a plate drop. I heard a couple of people scream. I heard a cup drop and tea splash on the thick red rug.

And then we saw Esther Rivas and London Bridges.

Esther opened her coat to show her gold badge and went to the woman in the blue coat who was standing and screaming. Lon came straight over to us.

"You've been leaving a trail," he said with a smile. "We got a call from the lady at Ollie's. We got a call from the pastor at the Our Savior Mission. Seems like you've been on a mission yourselves."

Lon turned to the nice man who introduced us to egg rolls and tea.

"I'll take care of the bill, Duke," Lon told him.

Darnell asked, "Who's Bill?"

"I think he means money," I told everyone.

"Ouch," said Tony. "Don't think we have that."

"There's no bill," said the man named Duke. "They seem to like our egg rolls. Just tell your friends to come back soon."

"Tomorrow?" asked Darnell. "Right after dinner?"

We heard the big red door slam shut and make a noise like a blast.

"I think you lost a customer, Duke," Esther Rivas told him. "Pull her bill and maybe we can charge her with a misdemeanor. Leaving without paying."

"Only if she promises not to come back," Duke said.

"We have to bring our friends back to where they live," Esther told him. "And consult with them about what they've found out about these cans."

Pilar held up her can of peaches, and I held up my apples.

"You can't leave until everyone has opened their fortune cookies," Duke said, and walked over to a bowl and filled his hands with things that made a crinkly sound. He came over and put them into our hands.

"Have you ever had fortune cookies?" he asked. "Sugar, flour, I think sesame oil—I'm not sure. A nice, sweet little taste. But the thing is—the message inside," he told us. "Crack open the cookie and take out the little slip. There's a message for you."

I think Duke didn't know that most of us couldn't read more than a few letters. But Esther just said, "Let me see them, too. You can't leave Duke's without getting your fortune."

Tony had already torn off the wrapper and cracked his cookie. He put the crumbs in his mouth and handed the small slip of paper inside to Esther. She read:

> YOU LEARN FROM YOUR MISTAKES.
> YOU WILL LEARN A LOT TODAY.

"Good one," said London Bridges. "That's me every day."

Darnell had nabbed the slip of paper with the tips of his fingers and slipped the whole little cookie into his mouth.

"It's good," he said. "Smooth. Sugar. Too small."

Esther flattened out his slip of paper and read:

"What's that mean?" asked Darnell. "I got a fortune cookie that I don't know what it means."

"I think it means when you're walking, you always look ahead to where you're going," said Esther.

"But I like just walking, too," said Darnell, and Lon reached out his hand.

"You got that right, too," he told him. "It's nice just to walk, and see what turns up."

Pilar handed the slip of paper from her cookie to Esther and listened while she chewed. This time Esther said:

YOU MAKE YOUR OWN HAPPINESS.

"How?" asked Pilar.

Esther Rivas thought for a moment, then told us, "You make yourself happy by being with people who make you happy. People who like and respect you, and you like them."

"I sure like you, Esther," I told her. "And you, London Bridges," I told him, and everyone giggled a little as I felt my face warm up.

"We like you. Like all of you," said Esther. "C'mon, Sal Gal. Give us a look at your fortune, won't you?"

I broke open the wrapper with a crinkle. I bit into the cookie halfway and let half fall into my hand. The fortune was on top of the cracked cookie pieces, a slim white slip on gold crumbles. Esther picked it up from my hand and read:

> A CHANCE MEETING OPENS DOORS
> TO SUCCESS AND FRIENDSHIP.

Then I think Esther's eyes got a little splash in them.

"I think that's really true, Sal Gal," she said, but talked to us all. "You get called out one day, go to some place you never thought of, meet some people you didn't even know about, and it changes your life."

"It changes you," Lon Bridges said softly. "Like you never dreamed."

Duke, the nice man who ran the place, told us, "You're not leaving here until I show you my favorite fortune. I keep cookies on hand with just that message."

He put 1, 2, 3, 4 more cookies into the held-out hands of Darnell, Pilar, Tony, and then me, and then turned around to a bowl and brought out 1, 2, 3 more.

"I'll open mine," said Duke, who ripped off the wrapper, snapped his cookie in his fingers, and read from the small, curly slip:

> STAY HEALTHY. EAT CHINESE FOOD.

"Words to live by," said London Bridges, and he put an arm around Darnell and then Tony, while Esther Rivas put an arm around my shoulder and took Pilar's hand.

"We've got to get you back to Sunnyside Plaza," she told us. "Dorothy, Mrs. Byrne—they're worried. And we've got to take a look at what you've found out about those cans."

We went through the big red door under the big, bright, red pig and saw the moon, big and gold, high above the city, and all the streetlights, like little moons, burning and glowing and showing us where to walk.

CHAPTER FIFTEEN

MRS. BYRNE WAS MAD BUT GLAD TO SEE US WHEN
Esther and Lon got us back to Sunnyside Plaza.

Dorothy cried. She said she thought she'd turned
around and let something bad happen to us and
couldn't forgive herself.

Mrs. Byrne said she'd got called in the middle of
the night by Dorothy and rushed over in her slippers.
She wore blue pajamas under a tan coat and shook
her head from side to side, over and over.

"Never, never, never make me...worry like that
again," she said slowly, with splashes in her eyes.
"Never, never, never, never."

Darnell, Pilar, Tony, and me could just say, "Yes," very softly.

Dorothy took us upstairs. She said we didn't have to brush our teeth and should just go straight to bed. She sat with me and Pilar while we whispered about the night and tried not to wake Shaaran and Trish.

"We went...everywhere!" Pilar told her. "We went to a place with fire in the window where they gave us orange juice! Boy, it was good."

"And the place with the nice lady and singing," I added. "We prayed. Usually people pray for us. But this time, they thanked us with a prayer."

"I forget for what," Pilar said. "And then—egg rolls!"

"At the place with the big fiery red pig!" I said.

"Sounds like Duke's," said Dorothy.

"And fortunes in cookies," said Pilar. "Like little messages. Mine said I could make myself happy. And Sal's message said meeting people can change your life."

"It sure can," said Dorothy. "People you don't know out there can change your life, if you let them in."

I think Pilar got quiet first. It took time for me to fall asleep, but when I did I began to dream. I felt like I didn't get to sleep at all. I was running, jumping, falling down, jumping up, and laughing. I don't remember much of what happened in the dreams. I remember they were loud and fun and colorful. I could read. I had a dog, named Chester, black and fluffy, and he'd play with my socks. Then I woke up, and when I woke up and realized the dreams were over, I felt a little sad but got up with a smile.

By the time we got down to the kitchen the next day, Esther Rivas and London Bridges were there with Conrad. They already had cups of coffee.

"Sorry, Sallie Gallie, but we couldn't wait," said Conrad. "Besides, I heard you folks had some fun last night. Figured you needed to sleep a little more."

I felt my face get warm.

"And we need your help," said Esther. "You can really help us just by being yourselves."

"Who else can I be?" asked Tony.

"You can't be me," said Pilar. "I'm me."

London Bridges had walked over to the door that we sometimes opened into the alley.

"Half an hour or so from now, George Nellos should ring this bell."

"The butthole," said Darnell, and London smiled.

"Let's try to keep that little nickname just between us," he said.

"He'll be delivering things," Esther explained. "Like he always does. Including cans. We've piled up some of the old cans he's already brought," she said, and tapped the tops of a few with her fingers. It sounded like tiny tin drums.

"Conrad will ask him, 'What's going on with these old cans?' We'll be in that closet around the corner," London Bridges told us. "Hearing every word George says, nice and loud, in our ears. Recording it, too. Who knows what he'll say? Maybe he'll tell us that he didn't know. Maybe he has a good explanation."

"But he has to think this is just like any other day," said Esther Rivas. "So maybe he'll tell Conrad what's been going on for so long. And that's where we need you to be you," said Esther. "Yourselves. Just working, chopping, running water, stacking bowls."

"When George and Conrad begin to talk, maybe you can walk just around the corner, too, one by one," said London Bridges. "So he doesn't think any-thing is out of the ordinary. But, Sal Gal," he said in a softer voice, "Esther and I think you need to stay here in the kitchen. With Conrad. Maybe turn your back on George, and be busy. You won't see him. He won't see your face while he's talking. But he'll see you, and think everything is normal. We don't want to leave Conrad alone. We don't know what George Nellos might do if he thinks he's totally alone with Conrad."

Conrad turned to me and put a hand on my shoulder.

"I need you here, Sal Gal" is all he said.

"And don't you worry, Sal," said Esther. "Lon and I will hear every word. We're just around the corner. We won't let anything happen. If we hear George say something we don't like..."

London Bridges made sure to find my eyes with his and look straight into mine.

"...something we don't like," he continued, "we're around that corner and on him in no time. Lickety-split," said London Bridges.

"Lickety-split," Darnell repeated. "I like that word. I like 'lickety' things."

We were still laughing and smiling and chopping and running water when we heard the bell on the door ring, and Esther Rivas said softly, "Places, everybody."

It all happened too soon for me to be scared.

Conrad had me fish for pear slices. Tony stacked bowls. Darnell ran a cloth across the smooth steel counter. Pilar counted out forks.

Conrad opened the door.

We knew George. He was a little shorter than Conrad, and he wore a white shirt with black pants under a short blue coat. He had 2 boxes in his arms and smiled as the door opened.

"Bring her in, George," Conrad told him, and George Nellos came in and stood up on his toes a little to put the boxes in his arms on the smooth steel counter.

"Ketchup and mustard," he told Conrad. "And I threw in a couple jars of pickles."

George said nothing to me, or to Darnell, Pilar, and Tony, and I was glad. Conrad had on his white apron and the white cap that made him look like a doctor and wiped his hands on a damp white cloth. He pointed to the pile of old cans on the counter and asked, "George, all these here cans. Look at the labels."

George Nellos asked, "What?"

"The dates," Conrad told him. "On the labels. The expiration dates. We ripped off the labels. The original ones—the real ones—are underneath, aren't they? Did you put on new ones?"

I could see George Nellos lift his arms up just below his shoulders and shrug.

"So?"

"Some of these cans are five, seven years old," Conrad told him.

"Oh, that means nothing."

I could hear Pilar put down forks, 1 on top of the other, 1, 2, 3, and then again.

"It means you shouldn't sell them," said Conrad.

"The stuff inside is fine," said George. "Good as ever."

"Says you."

"Look, Connie, you find one that's gone bad, I'll replace it," George told him. "No charge. But this stuff lasts forever. Every few months they find a can of peaches some soldier left behind in Afghanistan.

They open it up, plop it on ice cream, and have Peach Melba. No big deal."

Conrad kept turning the white cloth in his hands. He smiled but didn't seem happy.

"Now and then, yes, I suppose," he told him. "But some cans get a dent, or a scratch, then a hole. Or they stew in the heat and explode. Or just go bad. It doesn't matter. You're not supposed to sell stuff this old. It could hurt people. And a lot of people here can get hurt if they eat stuff that's old."

When George Nellos talked this time, his voice got higher. I'd never heard him with that voice before.

"What am I supposed to do, Connie? Just throw out all those cans? Throw away money like that?"

"Take them home and feed them to your family," Conrad told him. "If they're so darn good."

I heard Tony clack a last bowl into place and he went around the corner, like he'd been told. I lost my place trying to fish for pears with the spoon and told myself I had to at least look like I was trying and not listening.

George Nellos told Conrad, "That's all I'm trying to do, Connie—feed my family. Throw away those cans, I lose money. Sell them—I make an honest living."

"Honest?" Conrad asked him. "Selling expired goods?"

"Selling what I have left on my shelves, Connie," he told him. "Not throwing it away."

Darnell had run out of counter to wipe, and then he went around the corner. I kept my back to George Nellos, and I could hear the kitchen get more quiet.

"Sounds to me like an excuse to cheat people, George," Conrad told him.

"You feel cheated, Connie?" he asked. "I don't want that. Tell you what: We keep this between us, and I'll give you, oh, ten percent of the money I get each month."

I could still see Conrad, and he flapped his lips, almost like he was trying to spit.

"That's a bribe," he told George.

"A bribe is just a good deal, Connie," said George Nellos. "For two people who know the score in life. You served in subs. I was in the infantry. We're two people who know how to look out for each other."

Conrad wrung the white cloth tight in his hands. He pulled and stretched it and held it against the middle of his chest as he talked.

"George, the police are sniffing all around this

place," he told him. "We've had three folks get sick here. Two died. Another, Mary, a great gal, works right here in this kitchen—you've seen her—may never be the same. They're going to go years back and find out everything. Old food can cause them problems because of the medications they're on. It can build up and trigger strokes and heart problems."

I heard George Nellos puff out a long breath of air before he spoke.

"Well, I can't be responsible for what their meds might do, can I, Connie? I'm not Dr. Albert Schweitzer. I'm in the food business."

Conrad said nothing. I thought his face had gotten red. His lips looked flat and hard, like it would even be hard for him to talk.

"I could do twelve percent, too, Connie," George told him.

"Are we the only place lucky enough to get your old stuff?"

"I serve a select clientele, Connie. All these places want fresh stuff now, direct from the farmer's muddy hands. I can't give them five-year-old cans and take a chance someone gets sick. And I can't sell those cans to one of those fancy schools along the lake," George Nellos said. "They'd sue for sure."

"Our folks are people, too, George," Conrad told him. Conrad's eyes looked like hard round stones. "Our folks are just like—just as good—as anyone."

"Oh, heck, Connie, I know that," said George. His voice was even higher now. "And I love what you and the lady—"

"Mrs. Byrne."

"—right, I love what you do for them. I know they're people. Good people. But, Connie, what kind of lives do they have with their *challenges*? Or whatever you have to call it these days?" said George Nellos. "They look at the walls. They stare at screens. They don't know if it's Tuesday or Friday. The way they walk, talk, and draw. You see the scribbles of a five-year-old and think, 'Hey, another Picasso!' You look at the scrawls of these grown folks and think, 'How depressing!' I don't blame the folks, Connie. They're just *different*. It's how they were born. I'll bet if their parents could have known how they'd be, they'd wish they'd never been born. I know I would."

It was hard for me to look at Conrad. But I did.

I'd stopped trying to fish for a pear because I didn't want to bang the spoon against the side of the can and make a sound that would make George Nellos stop talking. I felt like shaking, but I didn't shake. I could see Conrad stay very still, and say nothing. Finally, George Nellos said something else.

"I'd even go to fifteen percent, Connie. If it would make you happy."

Conrad stretched the white cloth in his hands until his hands began to jiggle a little to hold it against his chest. I thought Conrad might tear the cloth in two.

"What would make me happy, George," he told him, "is for you to rot in jail!"

I heard a door roar open. I heard the sound of the city rush into the kitchen. Esther Rivas and London Bridges came around the corner to where we stood in front of the counter and the cans and the boxes of ketchup and mustard. They opened their coats as they stepped into the room and lifted their gold badges.

"George Nellos," said Esther, "we're Detectives Rivas and Bridges. Nineteenth District, Town Hall. We have a small camera and microphone right there—"

London Bridges had a finger pointed at a shelf just a little lower than his shoulders.

"—next to one of your cans of ten-year-old tomatoes."

George Nellos opened his eyes, big as baseballs, and just said, "What the...?"

"The recording goes to investigators from the health department, city and state," Esther told him.

"I'll get a fine," George Nellos told her. "At most."

"And then to the state's attorney's office," London Bridges added. "To look into criminal penalties."

"I'll write a check and be back next week," George Nellos told them. "The people who got sick here—you can't hang that on me."

"Once investigators and prosecutors see this"— and Lon turned again to point toward the tomato cans and the small camera and the microphone— "they'll hang everything they can find on you. Like a coatrack."

Darnell, Tony, and Pilar had walked back into the kitchen. They were quiet. They stood and looked. George Nellos stood silent for a moment and looked at Conrad. Conrad looked away. Then George lifted his shoulders in a shrug and turned. He began to walk away. He was reaching his hand for the knob on the door to go back into the alley when I decided I had to say something.

No, I had to shout something.

"I'm glad I was born!"

George Nellos didn't turn around. But he also didn't leave. So I kept talking.

"I know I'm *different*," I said. "I may not know if it's Tuesday or Wednesday, or how to ride the bus alone, or walk to the park by myself, or how to tie my shoes. But I know my friends. I know when people like me. I know when I like them. I like to work. I like people. I like to draw dogs and cats. I give them smiles, and they make people happy. I'm glad I was born. And I'm glad that I'm *different* than you."

George kept his hand on the knob of the door for a little while, and then pulled it open and left without turning around. We heard birds in the alley and another car and then a bus and then George's truck cough and begin to drive away.

Conrad held the white cloth over his eyes for a moment, and in another moment he came over to me. He put his head on my shoulder, and his white hat fell off and hit the floor, and we all laughed, me and Conrad, Darnell, Tony, Pilar, Esther Rivas, and London Bridges, and then Mrs. Byrne, who had come in. We all had our arms around each other and laughed until we had tears in our eyes and began to cough and then we had to laugh some more.

"I never laughed so much in my whole gosh darn life," said Conrad. "Pardon my French."

Darnell said, "I think I laughed so much, I wet my pants."

"You did," said Pilar.

We laughed and laughed again some more, and the laughs bounced and bounced off all the black pans and silver pots and the hard white walls and the shiny cool steel counter.

CHAPTER SIXTEEN

Mrs. Byrne had Dorothy bring new old clothes to Pilar and me one morning and said we should get ready for something special. She gave me a nice blue skirt and a red shirt and even a white sweater. She gave Pilar a dark blue skirt and a white shirt and a red sweater.

We got dressed and I told Pilar, "We'll match in different places."

We sat on a couch just next to where Mrs. Byrne worked, but she wouldn't tell us about the something special.

"It's a surprise," she said. "I can't tell you about a surprise. Or it wouldn't be one."

"Whatever you tell us will be a surprise," I told her, "because we don't know it," and Mrs. Byrne scrunched up her eyes, like she was angry. But I knew it was a joke.

"Oooh," said Mrs. Byrne. "You're smarter than me. But I still won't tell you. You'll know the surprise— well, two surprises, maybe—when they walk through that door."

"When will that be?" asked Pilar, and Mrs. Byrne scrunched her eyes again.

"That's a surprise, too."

"That's 1, 2, 3 surprises," I told Mrs. Byrne.

She just scrunched up her eyes.

Pilar and I sat and sat and heard the sounds from upstairs. Power-plus! Smooth and satisfying! Eight great locations all over the tri-state area! Fuel yourself all day!

There was a loud buzz that made us sit up, and then the door opened. Dorothy stood there with a woman who had short brown hair, very short, like a boy, and milky blue eyes. Then I saw...

"Mary!"

Mary.

I think she knew it was us, too. We looked at her eyes. She had new old clothes, too, a bright yellow coat, a white shirt, black pants, and new old red shoes.

Dorothy helped Mary walk into Sunnyside Plaza. She looked around but didn't move very easy. She didn't talk. But she looked at us.

"Mary can't speak. Yet," Dorothy told us. "Maybe later. Maybe not much, ever. But she hears you. She hears everything. She doesn't miss anything."

"Still Mary," I said, and took her hand.

"We'll bring Mary upstairs. To our room," said Pilar, but Mrs. Byrne shook her head.

"I count only one surprise so far, don't you? Stick around, what's your hurry?" she asked, and before we could think up anything to say or guess at another surprise, we heard the buzzer buzz again and Mrs. Byrne nodded her head toward the door.

The door rocked open again and stayed open.

Javvy came in first. Then Miriam. And then Esther Rivas, and then Rob Bartlestein.

And then London Bridges. And then Ferne Green.

"Mary is here!" said Esther Rivas. "Mary is back!"

"Cute new hairdo, too," Ferne Green said, and Mary smiled. She smiled and smiled and held my hand.

"I'll get Darnell, Tony, and Shaaran all ready," I heard Dorothy say, and then Esther Rivas came close to me and asked, "Can we talk for a minute, Sal?"

I sat back on the couch, and Esther sat on the long puffy arm of the couch and put a hand on my arm. She came even a little closer and kept her voice low.

"I don't know what will happen with...that... *guy*. George Nellos," she said. "But I know that whatever happens, he won't be able to do what he did to anyone again. You cracked the case. You figured it out. You, Sal Gal," she said. "And Pilar, Darnell, Tony—all of you."

"George is different," I told her. "Not nice."

"That's right for sure," said Esther. "And one of the things—one of the many things—I like about you is the way people can be nicer just by meeting you. With all that goes on in your world, Sal—how many times you might be annoyed at something you can't do, or don't understand—and you stay so nice. You can do so much, and understand so much. Especially people."

Then Esther squeezed my shoulder.

"I admire you, Sal Gal," she said.

"I...I...," I didn't know what to say. But Rob Bartlestein came over and leaned down over Esther's shoulder.

"Hello, Rob Bartlestein," she said with a smile. Rob Bartlestein smiled back.

"We thought we'd go to another ball game today, Sal," he said. "You and Pilar—and Mary. We play the Dodgers this time. We should have called to ask, but we wanted to surprise you."

"Yes, yes, yes," I told him.

Javvy came over and said, "You can help us keep score, Sal Gal."

"You remember the hot dogs?" asked Miriam.

Pilar said, "I've never been to a baseball game," and I told her, "Don't worry. I'll show you. I'll show you everything to do. The whole story is on the big green board."

"Lon and Ferne are going to take Darnell, Tony, and Shaaran, too," said Esther. "We got seats together."

"Darnell will have hot dogs," I told her. "1, 2, 3."

"Well, that's fine. We'll keep cash handy. And after the game we thought—well, do you remember Peking Duke's?"

"The red pig!" I said. "Egg rolls!"

"Duke is expecting us," she said. "He says he's got lots of great new fortunes for you. And Lon and I—we've been talking to some of the other people at the station house. A lot of folks would like to come over and get to know people here. Mrs. Byrne likes the idea. What do you think?"

"If everyone is as nice you—and Lon—everyone will think it's great."

"Well, I think—and you and your friends taught me this, Sal—that sometimes life puts people in front of you because you're not supposed to just walk past them."

I said, "I…I…I…," again, and Esther just put a soft hand against my cheek. I could barely feel it, but her hand made me turn pink, I'm sure.

We walked out of the door of Sunnyside Plaza. Rob Bartlestein and Javvy were first, then Mary and

Miriam, then me and Pilar and Esther Rivas in a clump. We had to be careful trying to walk because the whole street was crowded. Everyone wore blue. Everyone was excited. People yelled, but happy yells. Hey, over here! T-shirts! Ice-cold! The train above the street roared and rumbled. Rubber shoes rubbed and squeaked in the streets. Windows were open and people looked out, leaned out, and waved, even though they didn't know us.

"What a crowd!" said Javvy.

"We've also been thinking, Sal," said Esther, "that maybe once a month or so, you and Pilar and Mary could join us and go somewhere."

"A game again?" I asked.

"Well, sure," she said. "But there are shows you might like to see. And movies. And museums. There's a big museum along the lake with dinosaurs."

"Aren't dinosaurs mean?" Pilar asked, and Esther smiled.

"Not these. They're dead and stuffed. Or maybe they're just big plastic models of dinosaurs. There are also big museums with pictures. And churches with beautiful music. And concerts. And parks and picnics. And sometimes, maybe you could just come to our apartment again. When there's a holiday, like Seder, or Easter, or Christmas, you could stay over. Or you just staying over would make it a holiday."

"With Javvy and Miriam?"

Miriam heard us and turned around from where she walked with Mary.

"You guys can stay in my room," said Miriam. "There's plenty of room. I'll move into the room with little squirt. And all his smelly socks, *eeew*," she added. "If we're lucky, our father will make pancakes in the morning. From a mix, so he doesn't get too inventive. Like with walnuts or corn or cantaloupe."

"That was an awful invention," said Esther. "I remember."

"And if you're really lucky," said Miriam, "our mother will drag herself out of bed and make chilaquiles."

Esther took the soft blue sweater from her shoulders and pretended to swat Miriam as she laughed. Miriam pretended to guard her head from being swatted, then held on to Mary's hand. Pilar and I laughed to see Miriam get swatted. Javvy turned around from in front of us all and held out his arms from side to side along the sidewalk.

"Boy, all these people," he said. "I've never seen such a crowd. We better get there."

"Yes, we sure should," Rob Bartlestein told all of us. "It's family day."

AUTHOR'S NOTE

WHEN I WAS A YOUNG MAN, I WORKED AT A HALFWAY house with people who were then unkindly termed "mentally retarded adults." Today, we say "mentally challenged," or people with "intellectual disabilities." I was a case aide, charged with seeing that the fifteen or so people on my list took any nighttime medications, brushed their teeth, showered twice a week, changed into pajamas, went to bed, and stayed there.

I took the job because it was a few blocks from where I lived and had convenient hours that left me time to study, read, write, and watch late-night television. I didn't have any ambition to become a caregiver. The more I did that tiring, vital, and demanding job, the more I was inspired to do something easier. I became a reporter.

But I learned so much from the people who lived in that home. They were gifted, lively, funny, and interesting. I was shaken at first to meet adults who, in many ways, seemed to talk and act a little like children. But the more I got to know the residents, the less I saw them as people with mental challenges or disabilities, but real people who laughed, worried, loved, and made real lives in the world. They were direct, kind, and loving. I admired them.

I think of this story as a long-delayed thank-you to those people who became my friends and teachers. I have worked some of their names and personalities into this story, but it is a work of fiction.

While Sunnyside Plaza is inspired by the home in which I worked, today there are many different kinds of facilities for people with developmental disabilities, each with different policies and routines. I am especially impressed by the L'Arche communities, founded by the Catholic activist Jean Vanier, who says their goal is "listening to people with their pain, their joy, their hope, their history, listening to their heartbeats."

Our friends Don Kelly and Kathy Doan, who run a L'Arche house in Washington, DC, have read this story and offered advice, based on their experience. But Sunnyside Plaza is not a L'Arche community. Dr. Neil Cherian of Cleveland Clinic has advised me about medications and consequences, but the play of events in *Sunnyside Plaza* should not be taken as some kind of prescription. Different states have different rules and policies about drug treatments in communities for people with developmental disabilities, and those regimens described in *Sunnyside Plaza* should not be taken as standard across the country. Martin Oberman, attorney at law and former Cook County prosecutor and Chicago alderman, has read this story and advised on legal aspects.

I have also had expert advice on the interests of young readers from Elise and Paulina Simon, and Adelaide Machado-Ulm.

But all mistakes are mine, and mine alone.

SSS

ACKNOWLEDGMENTS

Thanks to Wayne Kabak; Alvina Ling and Ruqayyah Daud at Little, Brown; and to my friends from years ago at the Approved Home on Wilson Avenue, for opening my heart in so many ways.

Thanks to Elise Simon and Paulina Simon for making me want to write something worthwhile.

And, in a way, every word I write is for Caroline.

DISCUSSION GUIDE

1. How does Sally perceive the world around her? What examples can you think of where she takes in the world around her through the five senses?

2. How do children react to meeting Sally and the other residents of Sunnyside Plaza? Do those reactions change based on the behavior of the adults around them. If so, how?

3. At the Seder, everyone discusses the destinations of the Hebrews and other refugees. Who else in the book finds a new home or life? How do different cultures come together throughout the book?

4. Conrad explains to Sally that "sometimes, much as we love them, ... we just aren't the best people to be able to help the people we love" (p. 119). What different kinds of caregiving are discussed throughout the book? What does Sally think of her mother?

5. At each stop on their journey to the police station, the residents of Sunnyside Plaza encounter different types of people. How do these people engage with the residents? What behaviors do you think make Sally and her friends feel welcome?

6. How do the residents of Sunnyside Plaza work together? What strengths do they each bring to the table?

7. What does "family" mean to the residents of Sunnyside Plaza? How does this definition change over the course of the book?

8. Sally is confronted with death and dying several times throughout the book. How does she cope with death? How do she and the other residents of Sunnyside Plaza grapple with what comes after death?

9. Sally maintains a very open and welcoming personality. What examples can you think of where Sally makes other people feel more comfortable? What other ways does she impact the people around her?

10. Esther tells Sally that "sometimes life puts people in front of you because you're not supposed to just walk past them" (p. 189). Which characters in the book best illustrate this idea? How can you practice this in your daily life?